Ocotillo had been settled by proud men. Chief among them was probably Farris Rand, the High Sheriff of Mogollon County, but humility was in short supply all around. Hannah Early had never been known to step off the sidewalk to let respectable ladies pass. Abner Dinwiddie never closed his mouth, ever, anywhere. Clyde Littlejack, the village blacksmith, was too proud to admit how stupid he was. Even Billy Cordell was proud, although he was not an important man, not even to himself. Billy Cordell was another kind of Texan—not cattleman, not gunman, but simply wild man.

These peculiar citizens of Ocotillo recognized, by instinct, that they needed their peculiar town.

Also by Brian Garfield
Published by Ballantine Books:

BUGLE AND SPUR

Arizona

Brian Garfield

BALLANTINE BOOKS • NEW YORK

All rights reserved under International and Pan-American Copy-
right Conventions. Published in the United States by Ballantine
Books, a division of Random House, Inc., New York, and simul-
taneously in Canada by Random House of Canada, Limited, Tor-
onto, Canada.

ISBN 0-345-33572-4

Manufactured in the United States of America

First Edition: February 1969
Third Printing: August 1986

Chapter I

SOUTH of the Grand Canyon the plateau glides toward California. Across this sudden country of heroic proportions, Irishmen and Cornishmen and coolies in pantaloons and pigtails laid down the Santa Fe rails in '85, throwing open to settlement a vast grassland.

The sweeping Mogollon pastures became refuge and retreat for the last of the armadillo cattlemen, those crusty brawling Texans who had erupted into the West with a volcanic flow of cantankerous cattle. By 1870 they felt overcrowded in Texas; by 1880 the central West and Montana filled up; by 1890 there remained only Wyoming, Arizona, and the Indian Territory in Oklahoma. But the sodbusters, emboldened by farmers' laws, crouched around the edges of Oklahoma like hungry camp dogs around a tent, waiting for scraps. Land barons moved their sprawling herds into Wyoming, pickings for Butch Cassidy's Wild Bunch. And only Arizona remained open for the taking.

The armadillo rancher was not an old man, but the young West grew too fast for him. Trail-driving across the Red was only a recollection to be revived over a jug of sour mash. A man weaned on thicket beating, his teeth cut on thousand-mile trail driving, was a man who felt crowded when his nearest neighbor settled within twenty-five miles. He had grown up in a place where he could sit his saddle, look in any direction, and see nothing but cobalt sky across two hundred thousand unobstructed acres—and not a single plume of smoke in sight.

In the Mogollon country the grass remained free. Denying

5

the times, the cattlemen moved into Arizona on horseback, making the long drives from home for the last time. Brown-bellied cattle worked their way up every hillside and canyon, spreading across the virgin yellowgrass, and a mossyhorn Texan could stand on his front porch and survey a panorama that might have been the Texas of his youth—untrammeled, unordered, unsettled, and unlawed.

Might have been, but was not. While the East turned out its Boss Tweeds, the West put on long pants. By 1895 gas lamps and Ediphones had found their way into the Mogollon grass country. Barbed wire appeared. A telephone line ran from Mogollon Junction to the post office at Ocotillo, and the longest cattle drive anyone had to make was from Paria-ville to Williams Junction—a distance of one hundred miles.

Clay Rand lived in Ocotillo, and he was not a cowboy, but he rode in the roundup of '96 and ate dust in the drag on the trail drive from Pariaville. He was not especially needed on the drive. But his father was High Sheriff of Mogollon County, and Clay had turned nineteen, and his father said it would make a man of him.

Sheriff Rand was neither Texan nor cattleman. That did not matter; he was the High Sheriff, perhaps the most important official of all in the county seat at Ocotillo.

Ocotillo was the Spanish word for coach whip. Capt. Ed Partridge, the first Texan to settle in the valley, had followed his great herd like an Arab nomad. He had moved from the Pecos country into New Mexico, and that had gotten crowded, and he had gone on west to Sonoita. West of Sonoita lay the Sonora desert which sprouted nothing but bleached bones, and Partridge's search for elbowroom turned him north. His only possessions were his cattle, then number-ing ten thousand, and his rope and gun. And one other thing: a small soft spot in his iron-hooped toughness, a soft spot for a living thing that Ed Partridge thought beautiful.

He brought that living thing with him from Sonoita, where it grows in abundance: the *ocotillo*, which is neither bush nor tree, neither cactus nor quite coach whip. In the spring its ten-foot-high stalks are clothed full-length in blossoms of brilliant color, like painted lightning bolts. Capt. Ed Partridge brought a wagon load of ocotillos north with him, up over the Tonto Rim into the high grass country.

Ed Partridge died in 1888, trying to save his cattle in the

blizzard. He left no heirs. The enormous ranch was duly auctioned by the Territory. In the end it was divided into segments and distributed among three dozen bidders. The smallest of the resulting parcels amounted to twenty-four thousand acres.

A community appeared, to serve the new ranch populations. It was called Partridgeville until the new county government was organized in 1890 and the citizens gave the town its permanent name of Ocotillo. Ed Partridge's beloved plants were transplanted to the yard of the new courthouse, but the severe high-country winter of '91 did for most of them, and the others were all dead by '94, when their carcasses were uprooted and burned in Mayor Foster's fireplace. The wood of the Ocotillo gives off a faintly sweet-scented smoke.

The founder of the town had been an itinerant trader who had called himself Simon Vermilion. Within six months of his arrival, his trading post had three competitors, and Simon Vermilion took to drink. An inexperienced horseman, he had the habit of riding home at night at full speed. In January, 1892, Simon Vermilion rode his mount to its death and was killed in the horse's plunge.

The citizens dutifully erected a monument to Simon Vermilion and went on building. Around the monument grew the settlement, as lonely and monochromatic as the land around it. By 1896 Octotillo boasted a population of eight thousand. That figure was reached by including in the census the considerable population of the graveyard, as well as a small tribe of Indians who came to town twice a year to trade and get drunk.

Fortunes in gold and silver contributed greatly to the economy; Ocotillo was the main point of supply for the mines of the Rim country to the south. But it was, in outlook and character, a cattle town. It was built to last; it did not tolerate lawlessness.

In 1892, the year of Simon Vermilion's death, a cluster of fugitive Jack-Mormons migrated from north of the River and settled a few miles from Ocotillo. Their scatter of dugouts became headquarters for a cattle-stealing enterprise that supported fourteen large families. A year later the Cattlemen's Association wearied of these parasites, and as a result Farris Rand arrived with his wife and sixteen-year-old son.

Rand, a former soldier, town marshal, and railroad detective, employed in his service a revolver with a weighted club-handle, and a deputy named Harry Greiff. Within a month the Jack-Mormon village stood empty, its branding pens razed and its shacks caved in.

Since Farris Rand survived this adventure, the town did not erect a monument to him. Instead, he was elected sheriff by a two-thousand-vote majority and immediately appointed Harry Greiff his deputy.

Born to a line of military officers, Farris Rand had behind him thirty years' experience as a lawman, most of it on the post-Civil War frontier. He had a rigid code and a steel-bound sense of duty; he was a proud man.

That hardly made him unique. Ocotillo had been settled by proud men. Chief among them was probably Rand, the High Sheriff of Mogollon County, but humility was in short supply all around. Hannah Early had never been known to step off the sidewalk to let respectable ladies pass. Abner Dinwiddie never closed his mouth, ever, anywhere. Clyde Littlejack, the village blacksmith, was too proud to admit how stupid he was.

Even Billy Cordell was proud, although he was not an important man, not even to himself. His disgusted face was shaped by a dour knowledge of life's endless iniquities; he had long ago given up trying to live and let live. Billy Cordell was another kind of Texan—not cattleman, not gunman, but simply wild man. By profession he hunted wild horses in the far mountains, but his avocation was drinking, and when he was drunk his arrogance became casual, so that he fought absently and without malice.

As for Col. Stanton McAffee, he was as proud as any and quicker to demonstrate it. McAffee was an *East* Texan, yet another variety of armadillo. He practiced law as if it were a piano with stiff keys—loudly, bluntly, and often striking wrong notes.

The people of Ocotillo were old-fashioned in the world of the mauve '90s. But Ocotillo sheltered them; from Ocotillo they could watch the world go by, on the Santa Fe rails, without being swept along. In 1895 high winds snapped the telephone line that connected Ocotillo with the rest of the country, and it was eight months before anyone troubled to repair it.

The peculiar citizens recognized, by instinct, that they

needed their peculiar town. For that reason they all learned to suffer each other, proudly but courteously, like rival stallions when the horse herd is endangered. Ocotillo was an 1870 town endangered by the 1890s.

The 1890s arrived in the spring of 1896, in the person of Philip X. Shoumacher.

Shoumacher came to town quietly with his quiet wife. He quietly took over the *Territorial Enterprise,* and at first he published it quietly. Soon, however, the temptation to preach became too much for him. With all the zealous righteousness of a reformed character, Shoumacher launched a crusade against Ocotillo's roughshod ways.

Like William Jennings Bryan, Shoumacher held his nose and jumped in bodily without testing the water. And like Bryan, he sometimes preferred a ringing phrase to a sensible idea. Shoumacher's ringing phrases almost always included the word "civilization," and that was unfortunate; Ocotillo felt it was civilized enough.

Friction caused heat between Shoumacher and the rest of the community, notably Sheriff Rand. Barricaded behind his printing press, Shoumacher prepared for siege, nervously confident that in the end the right would triumph.

Then, in the fall, another newcomer arrived quietly— young Ben Harmony.

At first it appeared that footloose drifting brought him to Ocotillo. Ben Harmony was a Negro cowboy—more accurately, a dark mulatto, one of many sons of former slaves who had made a place in the West. He had hired on with the Pariaville roundup crew and helped drive the Association herd to the Santa Fe shipping pens at Williams Junction. During those weeks he had met young Clay Rand, and at the end of the drive he had taken a job with Clay.

The sheriff's son had a quarter section of land outside Ocotillo and had taken his pay in the form of beef on the hoof. With his small inheritance he had bought breeding stock, and when Clay started home from the railroad junction, he had a little herd of cattle with him. It was not strange that he might employ his black saddle partner to help drive home his two bulls, eight cows, and twenty-six yearling steers.

In the beginning, like the newspaper editor, Ben Harmony arrived quietly.

Chapter 2

THE wind touched Clay's face. He could feel with his cheeks the direction from which it came, dry and warm against his brick-red skin. Thirty-six cattle waddled down the road ahead of him, docile and obedient after several days on the trail.

The wind, coming up from the long grass basin, was autumn-hot, but nothing like the raking saws that sliced the farther deserts. You could tell a lot about a country by its wind. Every breeze had its own smell. This one carried grass scent, the clean virgin smell of unbroken land. Somewhere in its particles hung a waft of flowing clear water that stirred his horse and encouraged the cattle to walk faster. Clay couldn't separate things out, but the smell of this wind was unique; you couldn't mistake it: the smell of home.

Ben Harmony pulled off the road ahead and let the lead steer plod ahead, following the ruts. Ben Harmony waited for Clay to catch up. Impatience chased impudence across his dark face, and he said, "I thought it was only horses and cows that sleep upright."

"Aagh," said Clay, dismissing it. He wiped grit off his lips with the back of his hand. Bit chains jingled like coins in a man's pocket.

Ben Harmony said, "I see we're just about there."

"How do you know? What makes you so damn smart?"

"I was born smart, Chico."

Saddle leather squeaked. Hooves kicked up tufts of powder; looking forward along the humping backs of the cattle

10

was like looking at a heaving river flow. Clay said, "You sure you never saw this country before?"

"Never did."

"Then how'd you know?"

"Maybe I smelled it," Ben Harmony said.

"You can relax. We've still got three hours to home."

"I can hardly wait." Ben Harmony had a dry, melodious laugh.

The wind shifted, bringing strong cattle smell. Beyond leagues of rippled satin grass, haze-blue mountains lofted to summits of perpetual snows. This was home country, and Clay knew every hill and crease after almost five years of growing up in the valley, but to a stranger it must have seemed all a sameness. Dark spots on the slopes were Texas cattle grazing. The heavier mass of the foothills represented dark pine groves, but here on the high plain the meadows ran on for miles without a tree. Almost twenty miles north of the road, made pale by distance, red-cliffed monoliths soared and loomed, the beginnings of the broken butte country, inhabited only by scattered Indian shepherds. But the Mogollon's uniqueness was not in its plains or in its mountains; it was in its sky. Nowhere else was the sky quite so vast. Its crystal dome enfolded the land, shading evenly from deep colbalt overhead to a mist of thin azure above the far horizons.

The coach road meandered along the easiest course, as naturally carved as a river bed. Deep ruts testified to the passage of freighters behind long tandems of oxen and mules. The crushed ground was deep and rich in color, rouged by portions of clay. Here and there a tiny autumn blossom made a dot of brilliant hue.

Clay threw his head back to drain his canteen. He worked his tongue around; he was thinking of the chili-pepper sauce Ben Harmony had persuaded him to eat last night at the way station. His throat still flamed. He'd had the feeling he could have belched and lit someone's cigar across the room; he was surprised his shirt buttons had not dissolved.

The cattle plodded earnestly toward the promise of water. A tired cow lagged, and Ben Harmony tapped its haunch with the tip of his saddle rope. The cow plunged forward indignantly and took its place in line.

They were good cattle, sound stock to start Clay's ranch. His grandfather, back in North Carolina, had died a year ago. Among the various bequests had been fifteen hundred dollars for Clay.

At five dollars an acre, not a low price, he had bought a quarter section of grass on the lip of Blind Squaw Creek. It was about three miles northwest of town, and there wasn't a single tree on the property. Brush clogged the bottoms around the creek, and it had taken him a week in the spring to clear the bank. He had only sixty feet of creek bank where the stream sliced across the corner of his land, but that was as much as he'd need for some time. When the time came, he would dig a well.

It was as if he'd hung out a shingle: "Clay Rand, cattle rancher."

He'd wanted to buy his stock from Udray, whose ranch was just across the creek. But his father had called him to his office in the courthouse.

"A smooth sea never made a good sailor. Your trouble is you have too many dreams and not enough muscle. Before you can play in the game you're headed into, you've got to learn the rules, son. Go on the drive. Build your muscles and learn a few rules."

Now, home from the drive, he had a few new muscles and maybe he'd learned some rules. He'd learned a thing or two about cowboying from Ben Harmony, that was for sure.

He said, "You never did say where you came from, Ben."

"East."

"Or where you're heading."

"West."

"Sometimes you talk a fellow's ear off, don't you?"

Instead of answering, Ben Harmony pointed ahead. "This drove of yours is about to pull freight for that water. Might be a good idea if we ride on up to the point and keep them settled back. Unless you want to give them exercise."

They rode around ahead of the little herd and eased onto the road. The cattle moved faster all the time, like a freight train on a downhill grade. They would hold until they got within strong-smell distance of the creek; then there would be no point in keeping them back. They'd been two days on the trail without water.

Ben Harmony lifted the flap of his saddlebag, took out a cartridge belt, buckled it around his waist, and settled the holstered revolver against his hip.

Clay said, "What's that for?"

"Peace of mind."

"You won't need that. Nobody wears guns in Ocotillo."

Ben Harmony was not looking at him. "Chico, this is one town I don't intend to arrive in like a whipped dog."

"You won't need it, Ben. I'd appreciate your putting it away."

Ben Harmony started to lift his reins. "Look, if you don't want me to ride in with you, just say so."

"I didn't mean that."

"Then say what you mean."

"What are you getting all bent out of shape about? All I said was—"

"All right," Ben Harmony said. "Forget it."

Ten minutes later Ben Harmony said, "Chico?"

"What?"

"You sure nobody wears a gun in town?"

"Nobody except my father. He's the sheriff."

"You told me that." Ben Harmony thought it over. Finally he said, "All right," and removed the gun belt. He rolled it up and put it away.

"Thanks," Clay said.

"Didn't do it for you, Chico. But I figure maybe I'll attract enough notice without carrying the only gun in sight."

Clay disguised his aggravation by hipping around to study the cattle crowding along behind them. He liked Ben Harmony, but when Ben Harmony looked at you, you couldn't tell what he was thinking. You had the feeling he knew a lot of things he wasn't telling you. He seemed easygoing, but he was neither indolent nor timid. He tolerated many things but never submitted to anyone. Even when he was angry, he seemed amused.

He was the color of a tobacco stain, square of face and tall. Clay had met him at the Western Division roundup camp. The segundo had hired Ben Harmony as relief remuda wrangler, which was a man-breaking job that nobody wanted. The wrangler had a peg string of half-broke horses, most of them from Billy Cordell's mountain horse ranch. Billy Cordell was not noted as a trainer. There was some doubt whether he was as tame as his horses, but just the same, Billy Cordell was too old to ride out a bucking horse, and the occasional Indians who hired on with him were no match for the wild horses Cordell trapped. The ranchers bought horses from Cordell because you could get a sound animal from him for thirty dollars, but you also bought the job of training the horse.

Trained they were, but every morning the horse remuda met the day's work with rolling eyes and rearing backs. No working cowboy had time to tame a skittish horse when he galloped into camp for a remount. It was the wrangler's job to ride the cussedness out of them.

A cowboy on roundup used up five or six horses in a day's work, and the Western Division employed twenty-three riders. It meant more than a hundred horses had to be combed out every day.

That had been Clay's first sight of Ben Harmony, on the third day of roundup when Clay had rolled out of his sougans, gulped down flapjacks and coffee, and lugged his saddle to the rope corral at sunrise. The head wrangler had his hands full with a pitching sorrel, and Ben Harmony had limped forward, grinning through the dust, to take Clay's saddle and disappear into the whirl in search of a mount.

One morning Clay saw Ben Harmony talking with hard hand sweeps to the segundo. Clay hadn't heard the conversation, but the gist of it became obvious as soon as the segundo nodded his head and Ben Harmony stepped into the saddle of a cutting horse.

That afternoon Clay had found himself paired with Ben Harmony in a wide sweep for straggling cattle through the tortured breaks of the Malpais country. He never found out what Ben Harmony had said to the segundo, but whatever it was had convinced the segundo that Ben Harmony was worth more in the hills than he was in the corral.

Clay was nineteen. Ben Harmony couldn't have been more than twenty-four. But he seemed to have been weaned in the saddle. Clay knew that if he could learn half as much about cowboying as Ben Harmony had already forgotten, he'd be ahead of most cowboys.

He remembered one spill. He had picked himself up out of the brush patch, and Ben Harmony had ridden up, leading the beast that had thrown Clay. A gauze of tan dust hung over the hot badlands. Clay said, "I couldn't help it. It just happened."

"Nothing just happens. You forgot to grip with your knees. Horse didn't know which way you wanted him to go."

"I've had a gutful of this," Clay said.

"All right. I guess you just can't make silk purses out of sows' ears."

"To hell with you!"

Ben Harmony had laughed at him. "Careful what you say to me, Chico. You've got your left foot and your right foot, and it's for damn sure you don't need any more enemies right now."

"Don't get your feathers ruffled."

Ben Harmony said, "I've got a lot of things I want to do in my life, and waiting a week for you to get back on this horse isn't one of them."

Clay fitted his left boot into the stirrup, tested his weight, and looked forward. The horse stood like a watch spring ready to snap. Clay gathered the reins and the saddle horn together in his left hand and held them in a grip a crowbar could not have pried loose. He pulled himself up onto the horse, thinking, *Twelve hundred pounds of blasting powder.* "God damn old Billy Cordell."

"Ride him, cowboy," Ben Harmony said, amused.

A little while later Ben Harmony had said, "We hired on to do a job, Chico. From here on in, when I tell you to do something you do it. You get slow on me one more time, and I'll be all over you. I haven't got time to hold your hand."

"Now just a goddam minute—"

"Chico, you're wasting wind."

Ben Harmony had put his horse forward through the mesas. They had found a spring-engorged mesquite patch in a hollow, where, in a fragile web of sunlight and shadow, the tufted shortgrass was broken down, trampled so recently that it had not yet sprung back.

"Cows." Clay knelt to poke a twig into a pile of dung. "Still soft."

"Warm?"

"How do I know?"

"Better find out," Ben Harmony said.

Clay made a face. He put the flat of his hand on the pile as if it were red-hot.

"And?"

"Warm," Clay said. He wiped his hand on the grass. "Horse tracks over there, Ben."

"Think of that."

"But they're going in the wrong direction."

"Think again, Chico. A man breaks the grass down in the direction he's traveling, but a horse does the opposite. Looks like somebody else took care of those cows."

Clay got back on his horse, talking in gusty curses, and Ben Harmony said, "Patient, ever patient, and joy shall be thy share." He was laughing.

"Shut up."

"How old are you, Chico?"

"Going on twenty."

"One foot in the grave," said Ben Harmony. "Come on, then, we've got a lot of badlands to comb out."

The days followed along. Ben Harmony shared his fund of experience casually, as if he did not know how valuable it was to Clay. Clay followed him around at night, listening to him spin yarns at the campfire. He learned a few things about Ben Harmony.

Ben Harmony had hunted the thickets for wild critters with oxen and catch dogs. For nine years he had ridden the cattle trails from Texas to Wyoming, drinking chili juice in his coffee and handling a hundred different branding irons. He had worked plains cattle and mountain cattle; he had ridden for big cattle companies and little greasy sack outfits. He'd hired on as a top hand with the Hash Knife outfit, which at that time was the biggest ranch in the world, but he hadn't stayed long. He said, "I had to change places with a white steer wrastler who couldn't see fit to work on foot when I was on horseback above him."

Leading the little herd down the Ocotillo road, Clay totted up all the things Ben Harmony had taught him, and he felt good because he was going to be able to show something to Ben Harmony for a change.

They turned the cattle off the road at Clay's new mailbox, led them over the back ridge, and turned their horses aside to let the cattle run by. You couldn't stop them now. They plunged downhill in an ungainly swarm, crowded through the open gate and beat a heavy track to the creek corner.

With the sun beaming brass, Clay swept up his arm. "Home, Ben. That's home."

Ben Harmony squinted through the rise of dust. His only remark was a grunt.

The quarter section sloped up from the creek corner, undulating across a half dozen low hills. Clay's fence staggered around the boundary. There was no shade anywhere. He said tentatively, "Well, I haven't had time to build a shack."

"You figure to camp out all winter and nurse these cows?"

"It's three miles to town. I'll live with my folks until next spring. I'll build something then."

"You're sure full of ambition, Chico."

They rode onto the property, pulled the gate shut, and pushed cattle aside to reach the creek. The horses put their muzzles down and drank. Clay got down, walked upstream to the fence, and washed his face. Cow critters ordinarily judged a man afoot with disdain, but right now the herd was too busy watering to mind him. Ben Harmony washed, got mounted again, hooked a knee over the horn while he smoked, and swept the place with his attention. "Might not be too bad," he observed finally, "if you've got room to grow. Who's behind you?"

"Rafter Cross. They'll sell me a few sections if I get the money up."

"Time enough for that, I guess."

"Sure. Anyway I'm running blooded stock, and it won't take that much land. I'm going to plant forty acres in alfalfa next spring."

"Dirt farmer," Ben Harmony said contemptuously.

"Sticks and stones," said Clay. "But I'll get me the last laugh—you watch. The free grass is all gone, and these old mossyhorns around here are pinching up already—give me a few years and I'll be way ahead of the game. The future of the beef business is in blooded stock and trough feeding. You wait, Ben, you'll see."

"Who are you trying to convince, Chico? Me or you?" Ben Harmony laughed. "You'll do all right, I expect. Come on, let's have a look at that town of yours."

They latched the gate behind them and went on down the road. When they'd ridden up the last long hill, Clay stood up in his stirrups. "There."

"That's your old man's town, is it?"

"Ocotillo for sure."

Weathered into the land's own color, the town crouched like a spider in its web. Planted trees shaded squat houses on side streets. From the hill the riders had an embarrassing view of the realities that stood behind the sky-braced false fronts of proud establishments.

Ocotillo hunkered in a litter of sunbeaten 'dobes and clapboards, haphazardly strewn like marbles across a grid of dirt streets. Curved rutted paths connected the town with close-by houses, dairy and chicken farms. Dozens of water pump windmills sprouted like dandelions; their wood blades stirred squeaking in the warm breeze. Planning had gone awry somewhere, for all the streets suffered a jog and half-turn near the center of town, so that the pattern was that of a checkerboard broken in half and put back together unevenly. Within the town entire blocks of land stood weedy and dusty. The yards and corrals of a freight business occupied three continuous blocks.

Ben Harmony said, "They tell me love makes a fellow blind, but it sure lets you see a lot more in this town than I do."

Chapter 3

HE was nineteen, keen and full of hope; his rich vision saw each day in its brightest colors. It was a good day. Homecoming, and he had proved himself a man—at the roundup, on the trail, and in the honky-tonks at the end-of-the-drive railroad town. It wasn't that he had ever doubted. But it was as if there were something he had to prove to *him,* his father, the old man, the High Sheriff. And his mother, too, for that matter. Maybe now she wouldn't rake at him the way she always had ever since he'd quit practicing the damn piano.

The two of them breasted the head of Partridge Street and threaded the main street's light traffic. Ben Harmony's quick eyes swept the town with interest. They had to stop while fifteen teams of mules hauled a high-sided wagon through an intersection. Stenciled in a faded crescent across the side of the freighter was the legend, "Dinwiddie Freighting Co." The skinner whooped and cracked the lash from his seat asaddle on the wheel mule. Way up at the point team, a youth on a pony guided the lead mules down the center of the narrow side street. There was a lot of noise and dust.

The long row of high second-story façades ahead was uniformly faded and chipped by the weather, though some were only a year or two old. Warped wooden sidewalks curbed both sides of the street, some of them overhung by slanted shingle awning. Five blocks ahead, at what had started out to be the middle of town, the red brick courthouse stood self-righteously in the street, introduced by the Partridge monument and the wilted gardens where once the brittle stalks of ocotillos had blossomed. Like a river meeting a stubborn boulder, Partridge Street divided itself at the central square, went awkwardly around the courthouse, and rejoined beyond.

Colonel McAffee, who considered himself a Renaissance Man, was, among other pretensions, a self-proclaimed architect. Any blame for the outlandish shape of the courthouse had to be laid at McAffee's door. Its porch was porticoed by four truncated White Mountain pines, painted white in the misbegotten hope they might resemble Greek pillars. Since two of them were crooked and a third was out of plumb, the comparison required considerable imagination on the part of the beholder.

Above the sad veranda two gabled windows perched slightly off-center, like raised eyebrows. It had not been planned, but as things turned out, the county jail cells occupied that second floor, so that the gabled windows were crosshatched by iron bars. And poised on top of the entire precarious structure stood a tile-roofed cupola. This curious bell-house had been conceived in Colonel McAffee's mind as a graceful apex for his alcoholically conceived monstrosity, but it had come out too short, so that the effect was that of a red caboose stricken with elephantiasis, and possibly derailed.

Its crooked gables gave the courthouse the appearance of a slightly drunk uncle watching his nieces and nephews at play, with an expression of tolerant amusement.

One nephew was the town blacksmith, Clyde Littlejack. Because his trade forced him not only to shoe horses but also to treat their ills, Littlejack proudly boasted the title "farrier," although he had never been near a book, let alone a college of veterinary medicine.

Casting an enormous shadow, Littlejack stood with arms akimbo before his blacksmith shop, frowning in a way that obscured his eyes beneath his brows. When Clay and Ben Harmony rode by, Littlejack's head swiveled, indicating his interest in their passage. Elevating his nose an inch, Littlejack turned his back when Clay offered a greeting, and tramped into his shop.

A grin touched Ben Harmony's face. Clay glanced at him. Ben Harmony was tall and black. All his bones were big. The sweat-browned hat rested far back on his head. His grin seemed too jaunty.

They rode abreast of the newspaper office, intending to pass on by, but just then the editor appeared on the walk and hailed Clay.

Shoumacher was bookish and gentle in appearance. He had pink skin and large, bulging eyes.

"Welcome back, Clay."

Clay nodded an acknowledgement. He never knew how to take Shoumacher's courtesies. There was bad blood between Shoumacher and the sheriff.

Ben Harmony ranged his horse alongside. Shoumacher said, "It wouldn't be the best time to ride up there, Clay."

"Why not?"

"Might be a little donnybrook," Shoumacher said. "Somebody robbed Dinwiddie's office last week, and your father decided the culprit was Deke Stovall. Stovall came out of hiding a little while ago. I assume he's had a few libations to work up his spirit. He's been looking for your father. He says he wants to straighten things out."

"My father's not hard to find."

"Possibly. But Stovall's been prowling every shop on Partridge Street. He started with the courthouse, but—there he is now."

Clay looked down the street. He saw Stovall, a lizard of a man, coming down the far side of the street with a cocky walk. Stovall was little, narrow from all angles, bony and graceless. He was carrying a rifle.

Shoumacher said, "Maybe you ought to come inside and wait."

"There won't be any shooting," Clay said.

"Knowing your father, I wouldn't count on that." Shoumacher's brief smile was that of a nervous man about to lose his temper. He pushed his shoulder away from the wall, looking poised, but then he relaxed. Deke Stovall had stopped to poke his finger in a cowboy's chest and ask a question. Shoumacher said, "Stovall's just like your old man. He seems to believe a gun in the hand is worth the world by the tail."

Clay said, "Stovall's a two-bit tramp. He won't make any trouble."

Shoumacher stood in the shade of the canted porch awning and watched Stovall walk along the far side of the street. Heat pressed down on Ocotillo. Stovall hung his arms over the half-doors of the Occidental and peered into the bar-room; then he turned with a snap of his shoulders and went on. He had a face corroded by anger. He looked soft around the mouth; he had the colorless eyes of a reptile. He needed a thorough laundering.

There was something grotesque about Stovall that was more than the sum of his features.

Stovall crossed the intersection corner-for-corner and came right up to the newspaper office. He regarded Shoumacher incuriously and pointed his face at Clay. "Where's your old man, kid?"

"Why?" Clay asked, spuriously soft.

"Maybe I want a strip of his hide." Stovall had a high-pitched, abrasive voice.

Ben Harmony hadn't said a thing all this time. Now his sudden laugh startled them. Stovall halved his crooked grin. "Something funny, black boy?"

Ben Harmony shook his head mutely. Shoumacher had shrunk back against the door. Clay said, "Don't pick a fight with my father, Deke."

"I can handle him."

A heavy voice rolled forward from the end of the block. "All right, Deke. Handle me."

Clay had to look over his shoulder. His father was coming around the corner. The heavy black boots, polished to a wicked shine, thudded the walk, heavy and hollow, like mailed footsteps in a cold stone corridor.

Ben Harmony murmured, "Coming in straight up."

Clay licked his lips; they had gone dry. He watched his father's fierce, proud face for a sign of recognition, but the sheriff's whole attention was focused on Deke Stovall, who stepped down into the street, pivoted his narrow body, and fingered the grip of his rifle.

Farris Rand's big jaw stood out, blunt. He wore a bottle-green coat—dusty, drab, shiny here and there from long use.

A man with an incredibly wrinkled face left the Occidental and came nimbly toward them. Clay had time for a glimpse of that. He recognized Billy Cordell, the horse hunter.

Deke Stovall said, "You look good, Rand, for a fella that died this afternoon."

Farris Rand lowered his big silver head and watched Stovall as he might have watched a black widow spider. He said, "What seems to be the trouble, Deke?"

"As if you didn't know. You been spreading it around it was me busted into the freight office. It wasn't never."

"Teamster says he saw you."

"He's lying."

"Suppose we put it up to the judge."

"Who's gonna believe *me*?" Stovall demanded. "Nobody seen me, Rand. You made it up 'cause you had to have somebody you could arrest, is all." He blinked. "A man can talk himself to death, Rand."

"I'm all through talking," the sheriff said.

Clay's mouth opened, but he curbed his tongue. He saw Ben Harmony smiling.

Billy Cordell arrived like a volunteer fireman, red-faced and out of breath. "Hold on now, Deke."

Stovall turned his rifle. "Stay out of this."

Billy Cordell might have been sixty years old, but he moved like a youngster. He crouched down and slipped a big knife from his boot. Sunlight raced along the blade. "No, Deke."

The sheriff took one pace forward and batted Stovall's gun barrel down. He reached for Stovall's wrist, but Stovall whooped and leaped back. His shoulder struck Clay's horse; startled, the animal jumped against Ben Harmony's horse, and Clay had to untangle that mess. Ben Harmony was laughing quietly. When Clay looked around, Deke Stovall was slipping away like a bobcat, with the sheriff's stern voice riding over the other racket. Billy Cordell thrust out his leg, tripping Stovall. Lips peeled back in a spasm, Stovall exhaled a blast of breath when he hit the ground. He rolled in the street, gathering his feet under him, and the sheriff pounced.

The billyclub-weighted handle of Farris Rand's revolver rose and fell. Clay heard Stovall cry out. The sheriff put his gun away, hauled Stovall upright by his shirt, and cuffed the man on both cheeks. The noise was like the flat of a cleaver smacking a side of beef. Stovall had a nosebleed. The sheriff plunged a fist into Stovall's belly, and Stovall sagged with a whimper.

Shoumacher stepped away from the *Enterprise* door. "That's enough, for mercy's sake!"

Billy Cordell chuckled with satisfaction. "Fine, Farris."

Deputy Harry Greiff's squat figure hurried up the street. Clay saw people knotting up in doorways, looking out anxiously, not yet sure the fight was over. Stovall was upright only because the sheriff's grip on his shirt held him that way. Stovall's belly lurched.

Harry Greiff said, "Why, howdy, Clay." He seemed pleased. He snapped handcuffs on Stovall and said, "You're under arrest, Deke," as if Stovall needed to hear that.

Stovall gathered himself together, tossing his shoulders up and in. He spat in the sheriff's face.

The sheriff hit him in the mouth. Stovall's head rocked back. Clay jerked, and heard Shoumacher's shout: *"No!"*

"Get it out of here," the sheriff muttered, and Harry Greiff towed Stovall away. Greiff looked back over his shoulder and said, "Nice to see you, Clay."

A gaggle of people crowded around. From his seat on horseback, Clay saw his father's towering silver head. His father's voice rode against the crowd.

"My fine people, you have nothing to do here. Go on back to work."

Someone was cursing in a numb monotone. Clay's father stood aloof; the crowd moved back. "Go on—go on," he said. Billy Cordell was rubbing his hands together. Deferential, almost obsequious, the crowd dispersed and the street cleared slowly. A speck of dust got in Clay's eye, and he rubbed it.

It was the first time his father seemed to have noticed him.

"You'll take a lesson from this, boy. A man shouldn't get mad with a gun in his hand."

"For God's sake!" Shoumacher breathed.

"Don't think about it anymore," his father said, ignoring Shoumacher but possibly talking to himself as much as to any of them. Clay dismounted, stiff in all his joints. His father gripped him on both shoulders; a smile cracked the hard blunt face. Conscious of his plunging Adam's apple, Clay slipped his hands into the pockets of his Levi's.

All he could think of to say was, "Want you to meet a friend of mine."

Shoumacher stepped forward, breaking in. "If I may say so—"

"You may not."

Shoumacher's bulging hyperthyroid eyes made him look like a fish. The thin hair was combed carefully over his pink scalp. Grim as a pallbearer, he steadied himself—he always seemed a little drunk. He talked fast, blurting: "There was no need for that display. You went inexcusably beyond bounds."

The sheriff said wearily, "Go away."

Shoumacher's voice climbed to a pitch that most men would have reserved for use during a stampede. "You had no right! You glory in it! It's madness. The sheer arrogance, the brutality—"

"Shoumacher," said Farris Rand, "you're forcing me to offend you."

"I am offended," Shoumacher said, stiffening up, scuttling back to his comfortable retreat of phrase-making. "The existence of an appetite is not an automatic excuse to feed it, Sheriff. You treated that man with inhuman cruelty, and there's no justification for it."

Clay's father had his eyes all but closed. "I guess you spent quite a time working up to that outburst. Maybe now that you've got it off your chest, you'd like to go inside and cool off?"

Shoumacher reared back on his dignity. "Is that the way you expect to answer the charges in my newspaper?"

The sheriff twisted the points of his moustache. "If you had a tenth of the reverence I have for the law, you'd be able to stifle your smugness long enough to see why I roughed Deke up."

"You're a fossil, Rand. You're out-of-date. The day's long gone for an all-powerful gunman to strut around with the Ten Commandments in one hand and thunder and lightning in the other."

The sheriff's face turned; it picked up the bright flash of the sun and seemed remotely bitter. At all times he had a touch of isolation about him. He said, "Maybe someday nobody will need my kind anymore, Shoumacher, but the time hasn't come. Until it does, like me or not, you need me."

Clay saw color rise to Shoumacher's cheeks. Billy Cordell growled. Shoumacher forced up a smile like a dead halibut's. "There's no talking to you," he muttered. "Madness— madness." Then, according to his bewildering intricacy of thought, it was time to end the interview, and he swept inside the office. The door slammed—and Billy Cordell laughed.

Chapter 4

HIS father turned to him, gripped his biceps, and tucked his chin down to look Clay over. "You look strong, son. Meat on your shoulders. Let me see your hands."

Clay took his right hand out of his pocket, but his father made a grab at his left wrist.

Clay's fingers shook. He had a rope blister on his palm; he hadn't wanted his father to see it.

The sheriff said, "I let your mother do this," but he smiled afterward.

Clay said again, "I want you to meet my saddle partner—"

His father glanced upward.

"—Ben Harmony."

His father blinked, and there was an instant's hard pressure on Clay's arm before the sheriff dropped his hand away; he turned on both heels to face Ben Harmony.

Ben Harmony sat on his horse loosely, in an invertebrate pose. He raised his dark hand gently, as if in benediction.

The sheriff muttered, "What?"

He drew Clay's horse aside by the reins and walked over to Ben Harmony. "What's your name, boy?"

"Ben Harmony."

"Ben Harmony," the sheriff said. His head went way back. "I don't like craning my neck to talk to a man."

"I ran into fellows like that a few times before," said Ben Harmony. He obliged by sliding down off the saddle. He was as tall as the sheriff.

Clay pushed past Billy Cordell. Red in the face, he said, "I told you Ben's a friend of mine."

26

"Then he's welcome here," his father said.

Ben Harmony said, "I wouldn't want you to go to any trouble."

"The trouble will be all yours," Farris Rand said. Whatever was in his face, it wasn't anger. He glanced at Clay. "Don't heat up so fast, son."

Billy Cordell, left off on the edge of it, spoke up crankily. "Whatever you-all gabbing about ain't worth the powder to blow it to hell."

The sheriff said in a lukewarm tone, "You just seeing the elephant, boy?"

Clay said, "Who asked you to put my friends on the grill?"

"Just a minute, son."

Ben Harmony said, "I'll thank you not to call me 'boy,' Sheriff." He kept smiling, but his lips were at odds with his eyes.

The sheriff said, "You're forgetting where you came from, boy."

"Am I?"

The sheriff seemed grieved. "You came here of your own free will, and I'd hate to see this town carpet the streets with your hide."

Ben Harmony glanced at Clay—a slow, brooding stare—then back at the sheriff. "I'm not your lackey. Don't talk to me that way, old man."

Stiff with injured pride, Clay said, "I wouldn't have invited you down if I'd figured he was going to—"

"Chico, don't let it bother you. Your old man's doing his best to advise me. He's got to keep the peace, and he doesn't want me to walk out of this town with my head in my hands. That's all it is. Right, Sheriff?"

Farris Rand said, "The town is open to you, Ben Harmony. You can ride away whenever you feel you ought to."

"You mean you're giving me the choice."

"Not mine to give," the sheriff answered.

Ben Harmony's grin was impudent.

There was a thin rime of sweat on Clay's face. His heart had been racing, and he knew he was confused beyond understanding. Not that he hadn't known there might be trouble, from white trash and maybe from Southerners like Colonel McAffee. But he hadn't expected it from this quarter. Thousands of colored cowboys rode the trails. Spread through Arizona Territory, the Tenth Cavalry was a Negro regiment. Dan Cruze's Terrapin Ranch employed Negro cowhands, and so did the Matador. Clay was fairly well acquainted with John Burgess, foreman of the Matador. Burgess was a Negro, and once Colonel McAffee had made a point of walking out of the Occidental when Burgess walked in for a drink. But Clay's father had never read out John Burgess.

His father turned to him. "Have a drink with me."

Clay glanced at Ben Harmony, but Ben Harmony had put his back to them, to tie up the horses. Over his shoulder he said, "Go ahead, folks."

The sheriff put his thick arm over Clay's shoulders and walked him up the street.

The sun burst through the Occidental's windows upon a wide room under a low ceiling. Along the bar men clustered, talking animatedly. Farris Rand's appearance had a disintegrating effect on the conversation.

He had a way of bracing his arms akimbo and rising three or four times on his toes while he took in a scene. Clay stopped beside him, just inside the door. The pungent atmosphere pressed against his face. He could see the prints left by the grip of excitement on each face. They had all seen his father cut Deke Stovall down to size.

His father steered him forward. A cowboy made a place for them at the bar. The cowboy seemed anxious to curry favor.

"Mean little scorpion, Deke Stovall, ain't he, Sheriff?"

Farris Rand said, "Step up, gentlemen. You're drinking with my son and me."

The cowboy poked Clay in the arm. "Must be proud of your father, kid."

"Sure I am."

The cowboy slapped his shoulder, hard enough to drive his rib against the edge of the bar. "Attaboy."

Clay didn't like being touched. He saw Clyde Littlejack coming inside, big as a house. Littlejack's smile broke out in a sea of teeth. "You look real fine, Clay." But Littlejack had turned his back when Clay and Ben Harmony had ridden down the street together.

The sheriff poured himself a drink that was double the ordinary size. That was, as much as anything could be, a

measure of the way Farris Rand lived. He smoothed down
both ends of his heavy moustache. "Drink up, gentlemen."

Clay hesitated, then reached for his glass. He drank it
down without making a face.

There were times when his father appeared to have eyes in
the back of his head. Ben Harmony was coming in. The
sheriff turned, light on his feet. "Next time you come up
behind a man, announce yourself."

Clay couldn't see what he was so nervous about.

When Ben Harmony walked in, Littlejack moved farther
down the bar, presenting his broad back. Then Billy Cordell
tramped inside. Billy liked to give the impression that he was
wild as a puma and lean as whipcord. Actually, he was an
old man with bad kidneys. He had a weazened, pickled face,
pitted by the scars of a hundred falls off bucking horses.

When Billy Cordell reached the bar, the sheriff spoke to
the bartender. "Take the gentlemen's hat, Scotty."

Cordell took his hat off. "I'll keep my hat right here, if you
don't mind." The best his scarred face could do by way of
expression was twitch now and then, as if to drive away flies.
He had a trivial white moustache.

Clay was used to having him around. Billy Cordell had
ridden scout for Farris Rand's company of Dragoons in the
War thirty years ago. Ever since Clay could remember, the
old wolfer had been dropping in on them, all over the West.
He always slept on the floor when he came to visit. Clay's
mother didn't like that, but Billy Cordell said soft beds just
crippled your back up. His water-blue eyes had a glaze on
them like sediment, from all the years of squinting at sunny
deserts and sunny snows. He was part Choctaw, he said.
Nobody knew whether or not to believe him. It was his blue
eyes that confused the issue.

Billy Cordell had been a hell of a drinking man once, but
now he sipped beer. The sheriff and Clay and Ben Harmony
ranged down the bar from him. The sycophantic cowboy had
given Ben Harmony plenty of room.

Evidently it wasn't enough room for Clyde Littlejack.
Littlejack was all the way at the far end of the long bar, but he
looked pained and crowded. Below the Seth Thomas clock he
worked his mouth around a shotglass, drank distastefully, and
said something to the man beside him. The man looked up in
surprise and edged away from the blacksmith.

There was a bass growl of steady low talk through the room, the click of bottles on glasses, the scrape of chairs, the slide of a beer schooner cruising down the polished bar top.

Billy Cordell gestured toward the backbar. "Drink up, ev'body. They's a new soldier for every dead one."

Littlejack chose that point of time to leave the bar and come down toward them. His breath was redolent of a distillery. His eyes tried to be shrewd. He stopped right behind Ben Harmony and lied. "The last black boy tried to drink at the same bar with me got himself a busted jaw."

Ben Harmony smiled. He didn't turn around. He said, "Then he didn't know how to use his fists, which is not my weakness."

Clay expected his father to do something, but the sheriff only glanced at Ben Harmony and lifted one eyebrow. Billy Cordell licked his lips and turned around and hooked his elbows on the bar behind him. Littlejack was in back of Ben Harmony with his breath washing down on Ben Harmony's neck. Ben Harmony said, "Shut your mouth. Your mind's hanging out."

Ben Harmony spun around, grinning. Littlejack made a fist. "If you lay a finger on me, black boy—"

"If I do, you'll remember it."

There followed the sheriff's short grunt. Ben Harmony said, "Sit down and breathe through your nose," to Littlejack.

Littlejack spread his feet apart. Clay's father said, "Whatever you want to start, Clyde, don't. Not with me."

About that time Billy Cordell slipped his knife up out of his boot, and the sheriff spoke out of the side of his mouth. "No need to fill the air with blood, Billy."

Clay said, fast, "Don't lose your head, Clyde."

Ben Harmony said, "Clyde isn't losing his head. He's losing his nerve." He laughed in his throat.

Littlejack didn't seem to know what to do. Ben Harmony relaxed against the bar. "Clyde, a lot of people don't understand me. All they see is the gracious, warm surface. But I'll tell you. Underneath I'm a first-class son-of-a-bitch. You want me to show you now?"

The bartender said, "Outside, both of you."

Littlejack snapped at him: "I paid for your whiskey, Scotty. Not your lip." Then he focused on Ben Harmony again, at a loss; everything seemed to have slipped out of his big hands.

Ben Harmony murmured, "Yes, Clyde, I *am* better than you are." He kept laughing.

The sheriff said, "*You* shut up," to Ben Harmony, and then to Littlejack: "Haven't you got work to do this time of day?"

Billy Cordell was cleaning his fingernails with the point of his fourteen-inch knife.

Clay gathered his feet to step between Littlejack and Ben Harmony, but it proved unnecessary. The force of the sheriff's stare drove Littlejack away. He wanted to get the last word, however. He stopped at the door. "I won't forget this."

Ben Harmony said, "I'll see that you don't."

Littlejack left, exasperated.

Clay's father turned on Ben Harmony. "That pegged you, boy. You're carrying a chip. You could have stopped that."

"Sheriff, it's just started."

Farris Rand said, "Do you want me to have to bury you?" He turned a shoulder to Ben Harmony and reached for his drink. He hadn't said much, but he had averted a fight.

Ben Harmony said, "What did you want me to do—crawl?"

Clay said, "You *did* kind of egg him."

"I never said 'yassuh' to a white man in my life."

Farris Rand said, "We'll carve that on your headstone."

"Look," said Ben Harmony. "I didn't come down here to make trouble for you or anybody. Like you said, I'm just seeing the elephant. But when I get pushed, I push back. Old man, that's exactly what you'd do yourself."

"Only next time you may not have me around to hold your hand."

"I never did have anybody to hold my hand," Ben Harmony said, locking his glance on the sheriff's.

"Maybe you didn't," the sheriff agreed. The bartender walked past in the slot, and the sheriff stopped him. "Scotty, spread the word. As long as this man's in my jurisdiction I want folks to keep their hands off him. And their tongues." He put down his glass and turned to go. "Son, you'd better go on home and say hello to your mother." Then he left.

Clay said, "Am I supposed to get this?"

Ben Harmony said, "Maybe not. Is he always like that?"

"I don't know," Clay said, and that was true.

Billy Cordell put his knife away in his boot, sadly. There was no telling which side he might have picked, but either way he would have relished the fight.

Chapter 5

WHEN Clay and Ben Harmony reached the street, the sheriff was climbing the courthouse steps. They watched him disappear between pine pillars. Ben Harmony's eyes continued rising, up toward the cock-eyed gables. He said, "I think I like your old man, Chico."

It didn't surprise Clay any more than the rest of the afternoon had. He felt cranky; the day's events had rebuffed him, left him standing outside feeling that he must have missed something vital.

One of Dinwiddie's many wagons came bumping along. Chains clattered in the ox-yoke rings, and the driver spat tobacco juice into the street. Dust stirred behind like a slow, heavy sea. It was not oppressively hot, but sand grit covered everything, and when Clay licked his lips, he felt his tongue scrape. The sun was west of town, and shadows flowed far out into the street, dividing the dust into halves of beige and gray. Pedestrians cruised the walks singly and by twos— bustled ladies under parasols, booted men under hatbrims. Two men came toward the Occidental talking heatedly, one being Philip Shoumacher and the other Col. Stanton McAffee. Something McAffee said stiffened the newspaper editor into red-faced anger—an effect seldom difficult to achieve, notwithstanding Shoumacher's pacifist persuasion— and McAffee waved his walking stick as he reached the climax of his argument. His voice, anything but mellow, was audible a block away.

"No, sir. No, no, no. In that capacity he's got no power at all. Obeys laws, yes, yes, enforces them, yes. But powerless—

powerless, sir!—to make the laws or change them. It's a menial office. No meaning to it, no authority to do what's got to be done. Wouldn't touch it. No, sir. Not for me."

Shoumacher said something Clay couldn't hear. McAffee roared, "Want no part of it, you understand? Want no part of it at-tall. Good day to you." Thereupon the colonel turned his squat, sack-bellied shape away and marched into a store next door to Littlejack's blacksmith shop.

Ben Harmony said, "Who's that old crow?"

"Colonel McAffee."

"What's he do?"

"Do?"

"Do. To justify his existence."

Clay looked at him. "Well, I guess he's a lawyer."

That elicited Ben Harmony's laugh. Down the street Shoumacher turned head and eyes to the front, came forward and worked up a smile. "Hello there, Clay." He nodded to Ben Harmony. Clay could just about see Shoumacher's hackles settling back down; the colonel had upset him. Shoumacher was easily upset. He gave Ben Harmony one of his uneasy smiles and said, "Well, friend, how do you like our misbegotten country?"

"I don't know yet."

"I guess I didn't get your name."

"Ben Harmony."

"I'm Phil Shoumacher."

Clay watched them shake hands, the editor's pale soft hand crossing Ben Harmony's hard black one. Shoumacher said, "I hope you didn't let that little altercation with the sheriff put you off. He and I've had a friendly argument going on for quite a time. That's all it is."

"Is that a fact," Clay said.

Shoumacher tried to look placating. "Of course it is. Your father and I just had a gentlemanly disagreement over the question of whether the gun is mightier than the word."

"Isn't it?" Ben Harmony asked, mild and amused.

"No. Never. Law's like whiskey, Mr. Harmony. Give a man or a town too stiff a dose the first time and he's likely to swear off for life. And when you put too much power in the hands of a man who thinks he was ordained to rewrite God's tablets—"

Clay said, "You're climbing a molehill. My father was elected to keep the peace, and that's what he's doing."

"Okay, Joshua," said Ben Harmony. "Drop some walls on them." He grinned at Clay.

Shoumacher never strove for freshness when the tried-and-true would serve. He said, "The winds of change are blowing across this country, Clay, and you're young enough to bend with them. When a tree's young, it's strong, but it gives in the wind. When it gets as old as your father, it doesn't bend anymore. I'd hate to see you harden in his image. Your mother agrees with me, you know."

"I know," said Clay.

Ben Harmony said, "You don't like the sheriff much, do you?"

"No, I don't," Shoumacher said.

"Why?"

"He's a butcher. Last week—you didn't know this, Clay—a wanted man called Voss, Pete Voss, I think—came through town, and the sheriff arrested him. Voss resisted, and the sheriff killed him. It was cold-blooded murder.

"No," Ben Harmony said. "If that was true, you'd have gotten proof and printed it and had him impeached."

"He claimed self-defense. The man didn't have a chance. And you saw what he did today to that unfortunate creature."

Ben Harmony said, "Seemed to me the fella had it coming."

"Then you're as blind as the rest of them." That was Shoumacher's judgment, and having delivered it, he left them.

"Just a pious wool-gatherer, Shoumacher," Clay observed.

"Maybe not. Fella like that can make trouble, Chico."

"To hell with him," Clay said. "Look, I've got to get home and show myself or my old lady'll skin me. Come along and meet her."

"Why," said Ben Harmony, "I've been looking forward to that."

"My old lady," was an epithet he never would have used in her hearing; in fact, he seldom used it anywhere. Maybe it took the sting off his youthfulness. He didn't want Ben Harmony to get the idea there was any apron-string hanky-panky going on.

His whole life had been a tug-of-war between his parents. Right from the start it had been a struggle to balance between them, but still it had taken him a long time to learn that he couldn't please both of them. If he went skinny-dipping in the water hole on Herrera's dairy farm with the other boys, his mother got after him. If he didn't go, his father got after him. A year ago when he walked down Partridge Street, everybody watched him covertly, and it wasn't just his imagination. They didn't laugh at him, and nobody said anything; they treated him with reserved courtesy—reserve because they only tolerated him reluctantly, and courtesy only because he was the son of Farris Rand. They avoided his glance when they could.

One day he'd walked down to Feldman's dry goods store with his father. Clyde Littlejack had come along with a dour face and nodded to the sheriff. Clay had swiveled around on his heel and watched Littlejack cross the street and disappear into the smithy. Heat clung to the ground like melted tar. Weathered Ocotillo town lay drab under the burning sky. He remembered it all: he had said to his father, "It's as if I weren't even here. He might have looked at me."

The sun slanted under his father's hatbrim and struck his bold cheekbones. "Maybe it is time," his father had said, "you learned what manhood is all about."

And his father had sent him to work for Udray on the Rafter Cross. Clay hadn't liked it much. Udray made it clear he had no use for him, was only hiring him as a favor to the sheriff. Nobody in the valley had too much respect for a kid who'd exercised his fingers on a piano keyboard instead of a rope.

He remembered the disgusted young cowboy who'd picked a fight with him. "Get on your feet, kid. Look like a man if you know how."

He knew how. But he'd made it home to the bunkhouse under his own steam—just. That weekend his mother had taken one look at him and shut her face as if he'd become a stranger whom she didn't want to meet.

That had been a year ago. He'd had the feeling the pattern of his life was falling apart like breaking glass. But to spite his mother he'd gone back to the Rafter Cross on Monday.

The cowboy who'd licked him had shaken his head in disgust, but after that there were no more fights.

Udray, the superintendent, didn't have much time to train fledgling cowboys. Clay had learned the slow way. But one day Udray had come along, a rawhide Texan whom Clay respected, and said, "One thing to remember, kid. Whatsoever thy hand findeth to do, do it with thy might." The resonant timbre of Udray's voice had echoed around in his skull for a long time.

Then he'd come into the legacy from his grandfather, and he'd bought his ranch.

Ben Harmony's voice startled him. "That the place?"

"Uh-huh."

His mother was in the front garden, clipping buds from the rose bushes. She didn't look up until the two horsemen stopped outside the picket fence and Clay spoke.

"Hi."

She looked up. A tentative smile hesitated on her mouth; she brushed a strand of hair back from her face. "Hello, stranger."

He got down and stood awkwardly a few paces from her. Her face was grave. She wore her full dark hair swept up and back; she was now and always a handsome woman, slim and straight. She dusted her hands. A smile spread across her face, and Clay tossed his head. "This is my friend Ben Harmony."

Something like a lightning shock seemed to strike his mother's face even before she turned and looked at Clay's partner. Ben Harmony shook his head. Her eyes grew larger, and her lips moved unconsciously to form words: "Hello— hello, there."

She stirred. "Well, then, why don't both of you tie up your horses and come inside? I imagine you'd like a cup of coffee while I get supper."

"Sure." Clay glanced at Ben Harmony and turned up toward the long porch. Ben Harmony dismounted.

His mother said, "Aren't you going to tie your horse?"

"He won't go anywhere," Clay said. "I trained him to stand ground-hitched."

"I see."

Ben Harmony came up. Clay took off his hat, and they

followed his mother inside. He could smell the mixture of hard soap and cigar smoke that always permeated the house.

In the kitchen he sat with both hands wrapped around the steaming cup of coffee. "Saw some antelope headed south," he said vaguely. "Looks like a long winter coming."

Her smile was whimsical, a bit mystical. Ben Harmony was watching her closely. Clay said, "We brought some critters back to stock my place."

"That's wonderful, Clay." She said to Ben Harmony, "Don't you like your coffee, Ben?" She seemed anxious.

"Like it fine, Mrs. Rand." Ben Harmony lifted the cup toward his mouth and made a little gesture in toast.

She turned away and began to arrange the cut roses in a crystal vase. Ben Harmony stared down into the swirl of his coffee. Clay hunched himself forward, shoulders curved over elbows, and thought of something to say. "I ought to get a place built out there. How'd you like to help me build it, Ben?"

His mother's face turned toward them. She was looking at Ben Harmony, who met her glance and said, "I'd have to think about that, Chico. Don't know how long I'll stay around this town."

"If it's Littlejack and those others you're thinking about, remember what my father said. You won't have any trouble."

"That doesn't matter," said Ben Harmony.

"I thought maybe it would."

"Chico, when I was fifteen a crowd of drunk cowboys pulled guns on me and made me dance, which was when I learned how to talk turkey to that kind. Clyde and the rest of them just don't count."

Clay's mother said, "You must have had a terrible time."

Ben Harmony smiled. "I've been working my way since I was eight, Mrs. Rand. You get used to a lot of things."

"Some things I'd think you might never get used to," she said.

"Maybe. We've all got a hard-luck story, haven't we, ma'am?"

She had returned to her arrangement of roses. But Ben Harmony seemed to want her to hear what he had to say. "Clay, here, he's had what you might call an easy time. Anybody ever call you Nigger Ben, Chico?" Ben Harmony tipped his chair back and flung an arm over its rim. "I never went to school. Smart Negroes weren't in too much demand. But I schooled myself, and I guess it wasn't much harder than the other way. There was a miner I met once—he tried to stop me from voting. I took him through the Constitution and the Bill of Rights, clause by clause. The first clause was a boot in his shin and the last clause was a rock on his skull. I voted."

His face had hardened up. Clay's mother was watching him, agape, and Ben Harmony seemed to challenge her with his look.

Clay said, "Wait, now."

Ben Harmony's hand flapped at him. "I didn't mean to step out of line, Chico."

"It's all right," Clay's mother said.

"Is it, Mrs. Rand?" said Ben Harmony.

She said, "You're a little brash for a young man."

"Yes, ma'am."

"But that can be excused, I think."

"I make mistakes from time to time," Ben Harmony said, "but I don't make excuses. No, ma'am."

She said, "You don't need to 'ma'am' me, Ben."

"I know I don't need to."

Clay plunged his palms down flat on the table. Coffee splashed out of his cup. "I didn't think this kind of thing was going to happen when I brought you here, Ben."

"You didn't think at all," Ben Harmony told him. "But you didn't bring me anywhere, Chico. I brought myself."

"Why?" said Clay's mother.

Both young men looked at her. She said, "Why did you come here, Ben?"

Ben Harmony glanced at Clay before he answered. Then he said, "I guess I'm not sure."

Clay said, "If I'd figured—"

His mother interrupted gently. "Why don't you go up and wash for supper?"

Ben Harmony finished his coffee and watched Clay's mother wipe the table. Clay's boots struck back echoes from the hall. Ben Harmony said, "He's a smart kid. I guess I should have spent some time in school. The only time I ever thought about it was when I wanted to get out of the rain. I used to

spend all my time hanging around a cantina in El Paso.
There was a Mexican lady, used to make tortillas slapping
them from this arm to that arm."

"What happened to your mother, Ben?"

"Scarlet fever," he said. "I was eight. She was a fine
woman."

"I'm sorry."

"What for? Everybody dies, Mrs. Rand." He stood up and
went as far as the door, where he looked across the hall into
the open parlor. His eyes studied the room with care—the
antlered head over the fireplace, the massive table, the gun
cabinet. He said, "Seventeen years since I saw that case. He
carries it all with him, doesn't he?" He pulled up one corner
of his mouth.

"Ben."

"Ma'am?"

"How did you find us?"

"That wasn't hard. Everybody knows Farris Rand."

"What do you want?"

He grinned at her. "I thought I knew that. Now I'm not so
sure. All I know is, I saw myself pitching a rope at a steer
one day, and I thought, you work yourself to death and when
you're all through somebody's got to take up a collection to
bury you. Got to be more in it for Ben Harmony than that."

He fingered his calfskin vest. "Every time I wear a little
hole in my trousers, I take it in both hands and rip it two
feet wide, so I'll have to get me a new pair. I never wore a
patched piece of cloth in my life. That make any sense to
you, Mrs. Rand?"

"Yes."

"But I won't beg for a thing."

"No," she said. "You're all too proud for that. I never
knew a man who'd beg. As if it were a crime."

"It is, Mrs. Rand."

She tossed the damp cloth in the bucket. "I'd like a word
with you. About Clay."

"You don't like him having truck with me. Gives folks a
bad impression."

She said, "You're in a foul mood, aren't you? That's not
what I meant to say to you. I want you to talk to Clay."

"I see." He swung the kitchen chair around and straddled

it, arms folded across the top. "Have you got the speech all written out, or do I make it up as I go along?"

"Don't fence with me."

"No, ma'am."

"And don't mock me, Ben."

"I know what you want," he said, "and maybe if I was where you are, I might feel the same way. But the Cheyenne have a saying—a man's got to walk out his parents' shadow to find the light. I got to know Clay some, and I guess I know what's on your mind. Let him find his own way. It's the best thing."

"That's what Farris thinks."

"Is it wrong just because he thinks it?"

She said, "Are you sure you're not saying that because you had to find your own way? Because nobody held out a helping hand to you? Because you don't want him to have things any better than you had them?"

"I'm sure. But don't ask me to pick sides over the boy, because if I did I'd pick his daddy's side."

She gathered herself; she moved to the window and stood in its fading light. "Do you know what I think, Ben? I think you're so very sorry for yourself because you had such a bad time of it."

"Am I?"

"I think you are."

"I've forgotten about it."

"You're a liar, Ben."

"All right. I'm a liar."

"And you won't help me."

"No. It would only get him twisted up."

She said, "You may be wiser than any of us. I wish I could know."

"Nobody knows anything for sure," Ben Harmony said. "But you're in the wrong part of the world to get away with what you wanted. You figured to make a city fellow out of him. Teach him how to play the piano and read poems and add figures."

"He told you that, did he?"

"Told me the whole town took him for a sissy until he went under his daddy's wing. No, Mrs. Rand. You can't make this country into something it's not."

"I wanted to send him East. It was only his father who stopped it."

"Rightly. Clay'd have been a bull in a china shop."

The sheriff tramped into the house—the door banged, there was a pause while he hung his hat in the hall, and then his boulder-square body turned into the kitchen, filling the doorway. He recognized Ben Harmony with a drop of heavy brows and was about to speak when Clay came down the stairs two at a time, fresh-shaved and crease-ironed in clean broadcloth. The sheriff cleared his throat. "Supper ready?"

"I've just got to set the table," said Mrs. Rand.

"Let me," Clay said, and went at it.

The sheriff appropriated a stalk of celery. He had fine white teeth that cut crisply. "You gentlemen plan to leave your horses in the street all night with cinched-up saddles?"

Clay had a handful of knives and forks and linen napkins in silver rings. His raw-burned face colored, and Ben Harmony got off his chair. He went past the sheriff, almost passing close enough to brush by. The sheriff said, "You haven't got time to stable them. Just loosen the cinches. Clay can show you the way to the stable after you eat."

When Ben Harmony had gone outside, Clay stopped bolt still with his hands full of silver. His eyes flickered from his father to his mother, and back.

He said, "Maybe I'm making a mistake, but I get a feeling both of you must have known him someplace before."

His mother said, "Ben used to live in St. Louis."

"When I was a little kid?"

"Before you were born," his father told him. "He ran errands for the Agency."

"The Pinkertons? He couldn't have been more than five, six years old."

"About that," his father agreed. "He delivered telegrams for us. I knew his mother."

"Didn't he have a father?"

"I knew him too," said the sheriff.

Clay's mother said, "It was a very long time ago."

The door slammed. Ben Harmony came in, laughing.

Chapter 6

THE sheriff alternately bristled and harrumphed, a sure sign he was taken aback and unsure of himself—and that, for Farris Rand, was extraordinary.

The sheriff addressed himself to his meal. He would not eat a steak unless it was burned beyond recognition. Clay watched and ate slowly with his mouth tight and spare. A green pea rolled off his fork and fell on the chair between his legs. He didn't know whether or not to poke around for it. Finally he left it alone.

The newspaper lay open on the sideboard shelf. Clay's mother said, "Aren't you even going to read it?"

"Waste of time," his father muttered.

"Shoumacher says you—"

The sheriff cut in sharply. "Philip Shoumacher is hardly a sound source of information. He's published nothing but lies about me ever since he accused me of false arrest in the McGivern case."

Ben Harmony put on a look, slightly amused, of polite curiosity, and the sheriff obliged: "McGivern was convicted on my evidence. I rubbed Shoumacher's nose in it."

Clay's mother said, "That was months ago."

"Once a man lies, he'll lie again." The sheriff glanced at Clay. "Never trust that man, son. He's full of high-sounding language, but he's got a wire down inside him."

Clay shifted his seat. He hoped he hadn't sat on the pea and crushed it on his trousers.

His father turned back his lapel, displaying his dull-gleaming shield. "Don't make any mistakes about that fool,

43

Clay. Shoumacher made a lot of noise about the way I handled Deke Stovall out there. Now let me tell you what happened this afternoon so that you'll understand it. Stovall didn't challenge me. He challenged the law. You can kill the policeman, but you can't kill the badge. It will get up and come after you, on another man's coat." The sheriff sawed into his steak; he seemed cranky. "We'll never get the kind of civilization that Shoumacher wants out here until every tough in the Territory learns to respect the law. All right—we'll never reform hooligans like Stovall, but maybe we can beat the fear of God into them. It's about the best we can hope for, no matter what Shoumacher tells you."

Clay's mother said, "Is that why you killed that man Voss?"

The sheriff's lips clapped shut and rolled up in anger. She gave him an arch look. Finally the sheriff said, "The only tragedy in Pete Voss's death was that he died without ever knowing what he'd been living for. He was just riding around looking for a place to die in."

Ben Harmony murmured, "So you obliged him."

Clay's mother said, "You didn't have to kill him."

"I didn't have time not to."

She gathered the dishes, stubborn in silence, and Clay got out of his chair slowly. He brushed off the back of his trousers and glanced at the seat of his chair. No sign of the pea.

His father said, "Haven't you got an opinion, Clay? You never say what you're thinking."

"You want me to pick sides between you?"

His mother had stopped to look back at him. His father said, "My God, boy. You can tell us what you think without having to draw up battle lines and alliances, can't you?"

Clay looked at Ben Harmony, as if for aid, but no one had time to speak. A fist drummed impatiently on the front door.

Clay went to answer it. His father reached the hall; Deputy Harry Greiff stood on the stoop with his hat in his hands. "Sorry to interrupt your dinner, sir."

"Not half as sorry as I am," said the sheriff.

The deputy was low and wide. He came inside; Clay stepped back. Greiff said, "You remember Jules Beecham, teamster works for Dinwiddie?"

"The one who said he saw Stovall robbing the freight office."

Down the hall, behind the sheriff, Ben Harmony showed up in the doorway with his napkin.

Greiff said, "Beecham's been drinking down to the Hereford Bar ever since you thrun Stovall in jail today. I guess the whiskey greased his tongue some. Now he's saying he was the one robbed the freight office."

"What?"

"Beecham was flashing a roll of greenbacks when I got there a little while ago. Cryin' in his beer. Seems his conscience got after him—he seen what you done to Stovall. He said to me it wasn't right, what happened to Stovall, because Stovall never held up the freight office."

"Beecham admits he did it himself and framed Stovall?" The sheriff reached for his hat. "I don't believe it."

Ben Harmony said gently, "Don't tell us you roughed up the wrong man, Sheriff."

The sheriff's head swiveled. "Shut your mouth."

"Yeah," Ben Harmony drawled. "Shut mah mouth."

The sheriff reached for his hat. "Where is he, Mr. Greiff?"

"Beecham? I took him over to the jail. I just come from there—figured you'd better know right away."

The sheriff went out, talking. "What did Stovall do when you brought Beecham in?"

Clay didn't hear the answer. Ben Harmony tossed his napkin aside and came forward. "Let's go on down. I'd kind of like to see this."

They went outside and cinched up. Down the street the two officers walked briskly, Harry Greiff talking with his hands. Harry Greiff was an unspectacular, easygoing Pennsylvanian with a hound-dog face. He had been Farris Rand's sergeant major during the War thirty years ago. Ever since, he had maintained the same relationship to his chief. He had been constant midwife in attendance upon the achievements that filled Farris Rand's record; he kept in his blunt, shaggy head an exact log of all Farris Rand's glories and successes, and it was a mark of his love and loyalty that not a single moment's envy had ever disturbed his deep worship of Farris Rand. Harry Greiff looked upon his chief as many men regarded God.

Clay climbed aboard his horse and led the way, going down Holliday Street and turning, hurrying, into Partridge Street.

The sheriff was a fast walker. By the time Clay and Ben Harmony had dismounted in front of the courthouse, the sheriff and Greiff had gone inside.

Clay stripped off his hat inside the building and started up the stairs. He could hear someone shouting: "If that goddam witness could prove me guilty, you bastards would find him like a shot. I tell you I was clear down in the White Mountains that night."

Clay reached the head of the stairs, right behind Ben Harmony, and turned into the jail corridor. His father and Harry Greiff stood outside one of the cells. A single lantern flickered on low oil at the far end of the hall. The bare floorboards were worn gray.

The sheriff stood in profile, regarding the prisoner. All Clay could see of the man was his knuckles on the bars. The sheriff said, "Wait your turn, Richardson," and moved along to a farther cell. He made a gesture with his right hand; Harry Greiff selected a key and unlocked the cell door.

Ben Harmony stood pinch-mouthed, watching Deke Stovall marched out of the cell, talking under his breath. His face was high-colored, bruised and angry. He tossed his head and began to hurry forward, a ragged little man full of injured pride. The sheriff took him roughly by the arm and hurled him back against the bars. "Stay put a minute."

"Christ," said Stovall, "you can't—"

"I can," the sheriff cut in flatly. "Anything I want, Deke, so stand there and button up." He wheeled heavily to the next cell. "Beecham."

Harry Greiff opened the cell door. The sheriff said, "Get up and come out here."

Nobody appeared. The sheriff walked into the cell and came out dragging a filthy man by the shirt. Beecham looked as if he had lice in his beard. He was too drunk to keep his feet under him.

The sheriff pushed past Harry Greiff and slapped Beecham lightly on the cheek. "Now tell me what you told the rest of the town."

"Huh?" Beecham shook his head, trying to clear it.

"Who robbed Dinwiddie's office?" the sheriff demanded.

Beecham's expression had been lax; now it became cunning. "What if I don't say?"

"I might knock you around a little."

Beecham swallowed. "What if I do talk? Do I get a deal?"

"Sure," the sheriff said.

"What kind of deal?"

"I might not knock you around."

"Ain't enough."

Harry Grieff said, "Twenty men at least heard you confess in the Hereford Bar."

"I was drunk. Hell, I am drunk. You ain't going to believe a drunk."

Deke Stovall's lizard eyes whipped back and forth from face to face, blinking rapidly. Harry Greiff said, "Then where'd you get that roll of greenbacks?"

Beecham flung up his arm. "From him."

Stovall said, *"What?"*

"Sure, Deke gave me the money not to tell on him. I did see him robbin' the place."

"You bastard!" Stovall shrieked. "I never. Sheriff, the son-of-a-bitch is lyin'. I never had no money to give him. I never been near that freight office."

Beecham said, "You was so."

Stovall jumped at him. Harry Grieff, ready for it, pinned Stovall back against the bars. The sheriff changed his tone. "All right, Beecham, suppose I offer you a deal if you tell the truth."

"He's lying," Stovall cried.

Greiff shook his head, and Stovall went limp, with a resigned expression of hopelessness.

The sheriff said, "That wad of paper money did come from the freight office. You both seem to agree on that much."

"Sure it did," Beecham said eagerly. He almost lost his balance.

"Then since the money's been recovered," the sheriff said, "Dinwiddie might go easy on you if you tell us the truth."

"Why me?" Beecham demanded. "What makes you think I'm the one ain't telling the truth?"

"If Deke had taken that money," the sheriff said, "he wouldn't have given it to you. He'd more likely have slit your throat if you'd been a witness."

"Goddam right I would," Stovall said.

Beecham's hands fluttered. "All right, all right. I busted into the place. I took the money."

"Tell them I didn't have nothing to do with it," Stovall shouted.

The sheriff said, "Well?"

"Naw," said Beecham, "he wasn't even there. But I had to figure somebody to blame it on, didn't I?"

"Sure you did," the sheriff said. He pulled Beecham erect and pushed him back into the cell.

Beecham said, "Hey, wait a minute. You promised me a deal. You said you'd get Dinwiddie to drop the charges."

"Did I?" the sheriff murmured.

"You bastard! You double-crossed me."

The sheriff swung the cell door shut. "How does it feel?" he said, and turned away.

Beecham filled the hall with oaths. The sheriff said something to Deke Stovall; Stovall threw his hands in the air and came away shaking his head. Clay stepped over to the side of the hall to let him pass. His father came down the hall behind Stovall. "If you're smart, you'll head over the mountains, Deke."

"You don't need to fret none about that," Stovall muttered. He stopped at the head of the stairs. "Do I get my gun back?"

"It's been misplaced," said the sheriff. "Let us have your forwarding address, and if we find it, we'll send it to you."

"You bastard. You'd squeeze out the last drop of blood."

The sheriff came ahead with three long strides and cuffed Stovall. Stovall stumbled back against Ben Harmony, who pushed him away gently, regarding him with no expression whatever. Deke Stovall growled in his throat, turned like a scuttling animal, and plunged downstairs.

Harry Greiff's hound face frowned. The sheriff said, "See to your duties, Mr. Greiff."

"What about Richardson?"

"I wired the reservation. We'll keep him here till we hear from the agency police."

The prisoner spoke from his cell. "Those redskin sons-of-bitches, you think they'd lift a finger for a white man?"

"Maybe not for white trash like you," Harry Greiff said. "But you'd better hope they come through for you."

Ben Harmony said, "What's he charged with?"

"Stealing a horse," Greiff said. He closed his mouth and went down the stairs.

The sheriff was watching Ben Harmony. Ben Harmony was grinning at him, impudently, toughly, and the sheriff said, "Did anybody ask you to come down here?"

"I had a right to."

"You also had a right not to."

Clay said, "Look," to his father, and then his voice stopped.

His father turned. "All right. What's on your mind?"

"Did you have to bat those two around like that?" It was not what he had started out to say.

His father said, "Not you, too."

"I don't know," Clay said. "But sometimes the way you treat people, I get to feeling you've gone so empty inside that you had to fill up the hole with that badge."

"You're talking out of turn," his father said angrily.

Ben Harmony said, "You'd better beg his pardon, Chico. Oughtn't talk to your old man that way."

The sheriff squared off to face Clay. "Everybody has faults. My job is to see justice done. Some days that makes me a hero, and some days it doesn't. You think those two tinhorns didn't get justice from me? Is that what you think? Come on, son, let's hear from you. No?"

Clay faltered. "I just don't—"

"Squeamish," his father said. "Grow up, Clay. You're my son—I put right and wrong in you, and I put backbone in you. Let's see a little of it."

"Backbone," Clay muttered. "Is that what it took to beat up on those two?"

"Speak up."

Clay shook his head. His father said, "I'm not playing tag with those hooligans, Clay. If they're scared of me, then they'll respect the law. That's what matters. Do you understand that?"

Clay said, "You make it pretty hard for me to believe in you, you know that?" After that he didn't wait; he hurried downstairs, feeling the fingernails cut into his palms. He didn't stop until he was outside by his horse, where Ben Harmony caught up and grabbed him by the arm.

"What did you do that for, Chico? Don't you think you could've picked a more private place?"

Clay's tongue probed his lip corners. "I don't work up the steam to talk to him like that very often. When I do, it just comes out."

"Like diarrhea."

"I can't figure him out, Ben."

"What you mean is you can't figure yourself out. You're split right up the middle. Your ass is sore from sitting on the goddam fence."

"Why in hell do I always have to choose sides?" Clay cried.

"Because that's your lot," Ben said roughly. "Your old man's dead right, Chico. You've about reached the point where you've got to show some backbone."

"Backbone. I just don't get it." He picked up the reins of his horse. Lamplight washed softly out of the courthouse windows. "When I was a kid in school, we had an old Mexican woman who used to come in every day from some grub farm up the valley. She used to walk all the way to school every day. I don't remember her name. The kids used to pick on her something awful—you know kids. The old lady's wits were kind of slow, but I felt sorry for her because she wanted to *learn*—don't ask me why—and she put up with every bit of it. She used to sit in one of those side-arm desks that was too small for her because she was pretty damn fat, and she went grinding away at the lessons. She learned how to read and write better than most of the kids. I guess she's dead now, but I remember her. That's what I always called backbone, Ben. I never figured you had to carry a gun around."

"Nobody'd argue with that, Chico. But it took guts for that old woman to make up her mind and guts to stick by the decision."

Clay was hardly listening. His mind was off chasing a memory. "My mother wanted me to keep practicing at that piano, as if I didn't have fingers like so many bananas, and *him*, he wanted me to apply to West Point. I never could make up my mind, so I bought that ranch."

He gripped the stirrup in his right hand and twisted it around, ready for his boot. "I guess I'm a disappointment to both of them."

Ben Harmony said, "Maybe not. Look, maybe what we both need is a little whiskey and a night on the town."

"I'd better get out to the creek and bed down those cattle."

"They're tired. They'll bed themselves down. Those critters won't go anywhere." Ben Harmony flexed his muscles. "How about it?"

"I'll pass it up."

Ben Harmony shrugged. "I hope when *I'm* dead they don't forget to bury me." He looked up the street toward the bright lights of the Occidental. "You've been out herding cows so long your brains are dried up. You need a loose night, Chico."

Clay felt silly. He dropped the reins. "I don't expect to have a good time," he said.

"All right. Let's go out and have a rotten time."

Chapter 7

THE whiskey transported Clay's mind back into earlier youth, when things were easier, or so they now seemed. But you couldn't turn around and walk back into those days. Stubborn fingers on piano keys, knowing he was a third-rate talent; book pages by candlelight, poems by Burns and Gray and novels of Sir Walter Scott.

The Occidental bustled with trade—cowhands, miners, teamsters, shopkeepers, hunters, clerks, drifters on the way through to California or Mexico, and here and there a strange new face that could not be pigeonholed. Subdued laughter and talk, scraping chairs and the click of coins on card tables, and everybody keeping a resentful distance. The word had gone around, and it was as if Ben Harmony wore a sign on his back: "Do Not Touch, signed Farris Rand, High Sheriff."

Ben Harmony seemed to be in a sour mood. He said, "Me, I only drink to pass the time until I'm drunk." And later he said, "Remember this, Chico. Trust everybody if you want to, but never forget to cut the cards."

Clyde Littlejack was at a poker table facing the bar. His eyes were shrewd; they studied Ben Harmony with speculative scrutiny. Ben Harmony grinned brashly at him, and Littlejack fumed. Dinwiddie came in, wearing his stovepipe hat, and nodded amiably to Clay. Dinwiddie sat in on the card game, and Littlejack was heard to say, "The game is stud, and the stakes are two bits and four bits. That agreeable?"

"Just deal them," Dinwiddie said.

The Mexican guitar player came in from the back, pulled up a stool in the back of the room, and began to play. The quiet music filtered through the smoky murmur of the saloon. Clay watched the Mexican's hands scurry like spiders over the strings. There was more to drink; Clay felt drowsy in the room's dense, stale heat. A diaphanous cloud of tobacco smoke circled around under the low ceiling.

A foul word escaped Ben Harmony's lips, but when Clay shot a glance at him, Ben Harmony's eyes were flashing with wicked hilarity. When he met Clay's glance, he said, "Never mind, Chico. I'm only as drunk as I want to be."

"The hell time's it?" Clay muttered. He reached for his glass and emptied the dregs down his throat. The guitar strummed listlessly. "Let's go, huh?"

When he hit the open air, it revived him. Ben Harmony said, "Where to?"

Clay shrugged elaborately. A cowboy turned the corner with his head thrown back, howling a song.

Ben Harmony said, "Hello there, Vestry."

The cowboy looked down from the sky, got his bearings and grinned. "Ben!" In his enthusiasm he swarmed all over Ben Harmony. "Ain't seen you in a—I mean, a dog's age."

"You mean a coon's age, don't you?"

"Sure. Sure I do, Ben, and no offense meant."

"All right," Ben Harmony said. "Like you to meet my friend Rand."

The cowboy swept his hand around in a grand gesture. "I sympathize, Rand. With this crowbait for a friend you got no need for enemies." He grinned loosely and took Clay's hand in an exhausted grip.

"Sure," said Ben Harmony. "You look all rode out, Vestry."

"For damn sure. I been to Hannah Early's. Still can't walk straight." The rowdy flavor of Vestry's grin was vital and frantic. "You headed down to that cathouse? Man, that Hannah, she looks like Andrew Jackson and one of her god-damn biscuits fell off the table and damn near bust my foot, but by Jesus she's built like a brick cathouse. She do bring it all with her, for sure."

"Now, maybe that's an idea," said Ben Harmony.

"And more power to you," Vestry said. He shook his head in amazement and wandered past.

Across the street in the storefront window of the Canaanite Mission stood a big hand-lettered sign, lamplit like a theater stage: R E P E N T . Ben Harmony grinned crookedly at that and clapped Clay on the shoulder. "Lead the way, Chico."

"I don't think I want to—"

"Nonsense."

"I'll show you the way," Clay muttered. He stepped off.

It was a flimsy building of doubtful tenantry, judging by its façade. In the entryway powerful raw perfume registered keenly in his nostrils. He heard laughter; he banged on the inner door.

Hannah Early began to smile, but then she saw Ben Harmony. "What's this?"

"An initiate," Clay said, pronouncing the word with slow care.

Hannah Early was outrageously homely. Her nose was too big, her mouth was too big, her ears were too big. But she had a splendid body.

She gave out a bray of laughter and said in a scratchy baritone voice, "Then you came to the right place, young Mr. Harmony."

"How'd you know my name?"

"Ain't nobody in town don't know you," she said. "Come on in."

Her breasts, as she walked back into the parlor, bobbed and surged inside her dress. Hannah yelled up the stairs.

The room was piled with plush-heavy mauve draperies and furniture stuffed to the point of explosion—a riot of colors crowned by an enormous baroque chandelier.

A girl trotted down the stairs, and Hannah said to Clay, "Mr. Rand, this is Sue. She's a fine girl. Sue, this is Mr. Rand. He's a fine citizen."

Clay said, "No, thanks."

The girl pouted. "Don't you want to be friendly?"

Hannah said, "Why don't you two dance while I see to your friend?"

Clay poked his thumb toward Ben Harmony. "Ben here loves to dance. He studied with St. Vitus."

"Really?" said Sue.

"My friend," said Ben Harmony, "you're looking at a man

without character. I'm about to steal this young prize chicken away from you."

Clay regarded him as if marveling at Ben's depthless depravity. Then he switched his glance to Hannah. "Why are you looking at me?"

Hannah said, "Why are you looking at me?"

The girl Sue passed Clay with a slow flirt of the shoulder. He heard Ben's Rabelaisian laughter. Hannah said to Ben, "You are wondering whether beneath all this gilding there actually exist any lilies."

"What?"

"Don't be afraid of him, dear," she said to Sue. "He's at least half human."

Ben Harmony said again, "What?"

Hannah addressed him. "She's no young child of the woods, Ben Harmony. You don't have to be slow."

Ben Harmony bowed and swept his hat in a low arc. "If you're free, ma'am—"

"I'm free," said Sue, fascinated. "I'm very free."

Clay turned back to Hannah. "Do you mind if I ask you a question?"

"Do you think you're old enough?"

He laughed a little. He knew he was very drunk. But the deep, rich color of the place didn't hide its flyblown character, and he felt wrong about it. He put his hand to his head and frowned. Hannah said, "The only cure for a hangover is twenty-four hours."

"Suppose I don't live that long?"

"Done yourself up proper, I see. What was that question you wanted to ask me?"

"I forgot. Is that a misdemeanor or something?"

Ben Harmony was stumbling upstairs on Sue's arm. He looked back over his shoulder. "Chico?"

"I'm going home," Clay said. "No, I'm going to see my girl."

"You got a *girl?*"

"I don't know. Maybe I do." He batted past Hannah. "G'night, Hannah." He went outside and waited for the door to slam behind him.

The lights of a carriage passed him, and a wake of dust hung behind. Clay teetered on the balls of his feet. Down the street he could see the glowing porch lamp of Colonel McAffee's house, indicating that the McAffees had not retired for the night.

He said to himself with great care, "I have not thought of her once today until now," and having voiced the thought, he frowned at it. But finally he bolted toward the place.

He banged on the door and listened closely, hoping to hear light, quick footfalls. But it was the colonel's boots that tramped forward, and the colonel's flaccid hand that opened the door. Nonetheless Clay swept off his hat with as much gallantry as he could gather. "Good evening to you, Colonel."

McAffee gave him the eye. "It is past eleven, sir, and you've had a few drinks, I see."

So have you, you old mealymouth. "Yes, sir. I guess I have. I was wondering if Lavender was home."

"She is not."

"Yes, sir," he said, and stood on the porch with his hatbrim clutched in his hand.

"She's gone to the school dance," the colonel said. He added casually, so that Clay would know it was significant, "With young Bob Rivers."

"I didn't hear about any dance."

"Evidently. Go home. Sleep it off. And find yourself a new girl."

Clay brought him into focus. "What did you say?"

The colonel's loose face was as stern as he could make it. "You heard me. I won't have my granddaughter courted by you."

"Why?"

The colonel marched backward—he never walked, he marched—and shut the door in Clay's face.

Clay's mouth gulped open, shut, open, shut. Finally he stumbled back off the porch and swam opaquely through the night. At the curb he stopped and shook his fist at the house.

McAffee was a blowhard, and his sentiments of the moment were not to be taken seriously. But McAffee had never used that tone to him before.

It must have been Ben Harmony's arrival that had shocked the colonel. McAffee never let anybody forget where he came from.

Clay thought, *the old hypocrite.*

In his claw-hammer coat and white hat Colonel McAffee
had tried for years to bring honeysuckle gentility to Mogollon
County. So far the voters had not seen fit to elect him to any
office where he might do any damage. The colonel had
compensated for this slight upon his person by designing
buildings (one of which, unhappily, had been built), by
practicing law after a fashion, and by almost single-handedly
assuring the profits of the John Vale distillery in Nelson County, Kentucky. Scotty of the Occidental always stocked six
cases of John Vale bonded sour mash, in case an Act of God
should delay the colonel's regular shipment.

Except for his clothes, McAffee hardly resembled the ele-
gant colonels whose portraits adorned his favorite bottles. He
was squat and round; his belly made a perilous arc over his
waistband. He spoke with a Texas drawl, but his dialect was
clipped, not flowing. What was left of his hair was non-
descript brown. His nose resembled a fiery toadstool, bloated
and veined. He seemed incapable of sprouting either
moustache or goatee; even his sideburns were perilously scant.
Some said he had suffered typhoid fever as a boy and had
lost all his hair and that only tufts of it had grown back.

According to his claim, he actually had been brevet colonel with the Ninth Texas, but nobody really knew why he
had come West and chosen to settle in Ocotillo, which
promised to be the one town least likely to benefit from his
persistent efforts to reorganize the primitive county legal
machinery. Law in the Mogollon district was of the Old
Testament variety, and most of the leading citizens preferred
it that way. McAffee and Shoumacher, in his way, seemed
almost the only critics of Ocotillo's feudal system of laws,
whereby almost unlimited authority was vested in the High
Sheriff, whose office combined the functions of peace officer,
tax collector, jailer, and justice of the peace. The sheriff was
empowered to arrest tax evaders and fine them on the spot.
And since this forthright system worked well enough, nobody
saw much sense to McAffee's stuffy protests of irregularity
and Shoumacher's catcalls.

McAffee had disclosed nothing of his past, other than his
place of birth and his claim to a colonelcy. Naturally his
occluded history had become subject to rumor and specula-
tion, and the less he disclosed of it, the more enormous
became the rumors, in light of the curious fact that his past

was practically the only topic known to man on which McAffee did not have a prepared oration ready for instant delivery.

He did not seem to object to the circulation of the monstrous rumors that surrounded him. He seemed to enjoy playing the man of mystery and was not beneath contributing sly hints. Once Dinwiddie had speculated that McAffee was really William Clark Quantrill, the notorious guerrilla border raider, hiding out in disguise. Although McAffee's physique alone was enough to scotch that theory, Clay had several times heard him in his cups mumble vague references to "Bloody Bill" and "Jesse and Frank" and other noted members of Quantrill's raiders.

The theory given most currency was that McAffee had been driven away from his ancestral manor in East Texas because of his weakness for whiskey—that he was, pure and simple, a remittance man. What lent credence to this assumption was that McAffee had no real visible means of support. His legal practice was woefully small. His architectural genius had gone unpaid—some said he had donated his courthouse design to the county because if the county had been forced to pay, it might have found an architect elsewhere.

Whatever his past, McAffee was a man of grim, if alcoholic, purpose. He came (he insisted) from a land of deep-rooted traditions and proud culture, and he intended to see that Mogollon County got the benefit of his background, even if the citizens had to be dragged kicking and screaming to the trough.

Unfortunately his hopes had gone unrealized, mainly because it was said there was no point in standing up and arguing with him face to face because all you could get out of it was a windburn.

She danced in a whirl of flaring skirts, laughing. Clay watched from just inside the door. She was stunning, red-haired; her hair gathered flame and flowed lawlessly around her shoulders. The dark green dress set off her hair and her big hazel eyes. As she twisted to and fro, it molded her buoyant figure. She looked new, fresh, like a fawn. She was dancing with Bob Rivers, and when she looked into Bob River's face, her intimate smile was as good as a kiss. Clay fumed.

The dance ended and the caller mopped his face with a bandanna. Fiddles and guitar tuned up. Clay made his way through the crowd. He stared at her until she blushed. She said, "Why are you staring at me?"

"You know."

The caller announced a two-step. Clay asked her to dance with him.

"I've promised this one to Bobby." She smiled sweetly.

"Bobby has something else to do right now," Clay said. "Haven't you, Bobby?"

"Look, Rand—"

Clay set his jaw. The young clerk muttered something and plunged away into the crowd.

She snapped at him. "That wasn't nice."

"You don't seem to get too far being nice," Clay said.

Suddenly she smiled. "You're late."

"Am I?" He danced with her self-consciously, at a distance.

She said, "You smell of whiskey."

"Yeah."

She laughed at him. "I won't break." He moved in closer, feeling the warmth of her legs moving close against him. The music was loud and the room hot. She was delicate, lovely, sweet-scented: he loved to watch her laugh. His stare unsettled her again. The dance ended, and he said, "Come outside."

"What for?"

"Maybe just to prove you're not afraid."

It made her laugh and toss her head. She slid her arm into his. He saw Bobby Rivers by the punch bowl, making a point of ignoring them.

Spooning couples occupied the dark corners outside the schoolhouse. To get away from them, Clay walked her down toward the river. It was beginning to cool down; there was no moon. He stopped by the bank of the dry bed, under the overhang of a cottonwood, and the girl searched his face with an odd intensity. She said, "I think it's dangerous here."

"I was only making fun."

He bent forward to kiss her. Her lips were still and stiff under his. He drew back; her fawn eyes laughed at him; spirited, capricious, she dazzled and baffled him. He was not altogether sure what it was that made him lose his temper.

"What the hell kind of game do you think you're playing?"

"Don't shout," she said firmly. "I'm not deaf."

"Do you think you can—"

"Please don't," she said. "Clay, we're just two people who met one day."

"And that's all?" he asked. He was incredulous. "After all the—"

She turned away from him. He reached out angrily and lost his balance. His foot slid out on the damp grass. He fell down, arms and legs going in all directions.

She laughed at him.

"I couldn't help it," he protested.

"You're drunk."

He got up and dusted off the seat of his pants. He could see one bright laughing eye through the soft tumble of her hair. She said, "I'm sorry. I always laugh in all the wrong places. I laugh at Greek tragedies."

"I'm not Greek. And I'm not so sure I'm a tragedy, either."

"You never know, do you?" She laughed again. He loved the way her face changed when she laughed. He regarded her gravely; he leaned toward her for a kiss.

She slipped her face aside once more. "You're supposed to give a girl a ring before you kiss her."

It made him retreat toward the tree. "What? You confuse me," he said. "Every time I see you, I get confused."

Her eyes were innocent. "Why, why ever should you?"

"A minute ago we were just two people who met one day. Now you're bawling for a ring on your finger."

A strand of hair fell across her eye, and she pushed it back. She was giving him a hurt, slantwise look. He said, "Oh, no. Are you going to cry now?"

"Not if I can help it." She sniffed.

"I'll leave. Is that what you want?"

"I don't know," she bawled.

"Oh, for God's sake, cut that out." He threw up his hands. "Will you cut it out? I don't know what to do with you when you do that."

She fished a cambric handkerchief out of her sleeve and wiped her eyes.

"Will you just calm down?" he pleaded. "Christ, the whole town will think I hit you or something."

In time she put the handkerchief away and sniffed once. Her eyes were puffed, and she wouldn't look at him. Clay reached for her hand hesitantly and patted it. "Lavender, the world has not come to an end. You aren't dead yet."

"I'm sorry. I didn't mean to do that." She fingered his hand. "I must look a fright."

He folded his arms. "The way you were looking at Bob Rivers."

"What?"

"It makes me crazy to think you ever smile at anybody the way you smile at me."

"I know." When she smiled, there was something held back, and he took a step forward. She looked down in embarrassment.

He said, "Okay, I'm stupid. Indignant and jealous. But it's just that I can't breathe right when I'm with you."

She put her face in her hands. He said, "What now, for God's sake?"

Her voice was muffled. "He told me not to see you anymore."

"Your grandfather?"

"Yes."

"The old goat."

"Clay—"

"Hell, he'll get over it. You know him. Tomorrow morning he won't remember a thing." He kissed her mouth, only a gentle touch of the lips, but she pulled him against her and he felt the fire-lick of her tongue.

She said, "Do that again."

He tickled her ear with his finger and stopped her voice with a kiss. She slipped her face away, guiding his lips down her cheek to her throat, and she said, "I'm not sure this time, Clay. He sounded serious."

"The old windbag always sounds serious, like an earthquake," he muttered. Lavender's red hair shone softly in the backlighting of the schoolhouse lamps up the hill. "Forget him," Clay said. In a tranquil state of mind he walked her closer to the tree and sat down on the grass. He gripped both her hands, and his words came in a headlong rush.

"I'm crazy in love with you, Lavender. I wish there was something nobody else had ever said before, some new way to tell you how I feel. I've got to have you to keep."

She sucked his lower lip. He wanted to lose himself in her. She said, "Clay?"

"What?"

"Does everybody feel like this, or are we very special?"

Chapter 8

DINWIDDIE's freight yards fronted on Holliday Street, several blocks of warehouses and corrals and stables. A high-sided wagon stood leaning on its braces in front of the place; two men in coveralls hitched mule teams into the spans. There was a good deal of noise from scuffling and cursing; there was dust in the air, and the smell was strong. Dinwiddie's operation ran around the clock, even late on a Saturday night, with numerous gas lamps blasting around like brass hammers. Dinwiddie, a night owl who seemed to survive on very little sleep, stood on the office porch with his arms folded and the stovepipe hat standing straight up on his head. He was watching his men hitch up the mules, and there was a caustic glitter in his eyes, but when he saw the sheriff coming into the lamplight, he turned with a piece of a smile shaping his sardonic mouth.

The sheriff walked wearily into the dust and profanity that clouded the big freight rig. Dinwiddie said, "Howdy, Farris," and the sheriff gave him a nod.

"Making your last rounds for the night?"

"Yes." The sheriff handed him an envelope. "Mind counting that?"

Dinwiddie stripped the envelope and held it up to the light curiously. "Where'd you get this?"

"Jules Beecham."

"Think of that. Want to come inside?"

"I'm on my way home."

Dinwiddie counted the greenbacks, and the sheriff said, "Come around Monday morning and sign the papers."

"Incredible," Dinwiddie muttered.

"Is it all there?"

"Almost. Maybe twenty dollars short."

"He spent that on whiskey."

"But what about Stovall?"

"I let him go," the sheriff said.

Dinwiddie gave him a dry look. "Good thing you hadn't already killed him, wasn't it? Like Pete Voss."

The sheriff's eyelids went to half-mast, and he began to turn away. Dinwiddie said, "Too bad Pete Voss picked this town to die in, wasn't it?"

"It didn't seem to matter much to him where he died. I don't see why it should matter to you."

"I'd just as soon he'd picked some other town to get killed in." Dinwiddie's smile tipped over to the side. "No reason why me and the other taxpayers should have to foot the bill for his funeral."

The sheriff said, "Voss had forty dollars in his jeans. He's paying for his own coffin."

Dinwiddie patted his stomach. "Well, now, that's different. I'm glad you told me that, Farris, because now I don't feel so bad about it anymore."

"Sure," the sheriff said. "Good night." He stepped off the porch and was absorbed by the night.

Dinwiddie went inside and put the money in the safe. He said to the night clerk, "Hold the fort. I'm going home." But instead of that, he went toward Partridge Street, keeping to the boardwalks to avoid dust where he could. It was his habit to have a nightcap in the Occidental before retiring each night.

When Philip Shoumacher had been seven years old, his father had boxed his ears so hard that Shoumacher had lost almost all the hearing in his right ear. It offended his vanity to have anyone know of his blameless partial infirmity; it was one of many secrets he kept close to his chest.

At thirty-six, Shoumacher was dried up and aware of it. His hair was thin; his skin was pink, and no amount of weather could toughen it; his eyes bulged unpleasantly. He had married the only woman he had found who would have him; the bargain was at best satisfactory. Sensitive to the inimicality of fate and the extent of his own limitations, Philip Shoumacher had early in life discovered Demon Rum.

This evening he had been drinking steadily for five hours. His eyes had gone vague, and he almost upset the glass when he reached for it. The Occidental was quiet, virtually deserted; he had the back of the room to himself. He stuck out a long index finger and swirled it in the glass. At his elbow lay a scratch pad and pencil. The top sheet was full of his lavish scrawl, but most of it had been crossed out with angry slashes.

He noticed Dinwiddie's arrival with no great pleasure, although Dinwiddie was one of the few congenial souls Shoumacher had encountered in Ocotillo. Dinwiddie seemed to share Shoumacher's solemn outlook, but the difference between them was that Dinwiddie glossed his with a caustic sense of humor that seemed to equip him to roll with any blow. One of Shoumacher's own weaknesses was a dearth of humor, and tonight he was not sure he was prepared to put up with Dinwiddie's defensive gallows jokes. Dinwiddie had been the self-appointed vocal conscience of Ocotillo up to the time of Shoumacher's arrival—the oracular voice to whom the saloon-goers had listened nightly. More than a pundit, less than a doom-sayer, Dinwiddie had provided satisfying entertainment until Shoumacher had appeared, to inject fire, vigor, righteousness, and rage into the pages of the tired newspaper. If Dinwiddie resented the competition, he had never made an issue of it; his impersonal grudge against the world was full and deep, but he did not seem to harbor personal grudges.

Shoumacher rather liked Dinwiddie. But liking, with Philip Shoumacher, was a shadowy thing. He did not have friends— only sometime allies. His backtrail was strewn with acquaintances and a variety of enemies stung beyond forgiveness by the vitriol of his tongue and pen.

There was, he saw, no way of avoiding the man this evening: Dinwiddie had discovered him.

Dinwiddie came to the table. Begrudging it, Shoumacher kicked out the empty chair. "Want a drink?"

"Do cows give milk?" Dinwiddie sat. He placed on the table his trademark—the tall black stovepipe hat. He was a sepulchral character, his face scored and gaunt, his hair plastered down like a brown skullcap, parted in the exact center. His expression was habitually derisive. "How many drinks do I need to have to catch up with you?"

"Innumerable," the editor said. "Innumerable drinks. But I can still pronounce 'innumerable,' so I think I haven't had enough." He signaled the bartender.

Without invitation, Dinwiddie reached across the table and turned Shoumacher's scratch pad end-for-end to read it. Shoumacher almost protested. In the end he said nothing, seeing the pointlessness of it.

"Every time you cross it out, you replace it with something more vicious. You really hate Farris's guts, don't you?"

Shoumacher grunted. Dinwiddie pushed the pad back to him. "You know, it won't help to go beyond bounds, Phil. If you want to fire up the people, give them something to think about—but don't hit 'em over the head with it. This kind of diatribe—hell, print this and you'll turn them all against you. Why not be a little more subtle about it?"

"I guess I'm not a subtle man."

Dinwiddie said, "Well, who cares, anyway? This damn roulette wheel we're on, never knowing what slot we'll fall into—how on earth can you take things so seriously?"

"It's a curse that was placed on me."

The barkeep served them and went. Dinwiddie made a wry toast and drank. He made a face. "Soap. It tastes like soap."

"Try another kind."

"They're all the same." Dinwiddie wiped his mouth. "Tell me something. Prior to this insanity, where'd you come from? What made you pick this God-forsaken town?"

"What made you pick it?" Shoumacher countered.

"My elder brother, may his soul rot."

"How so?"

"He dropped dead. This country killed him. Bequeathed to me the vast and powerful industry which you now see under my command."

"You didn't have to accept it, did you?"

"Of course I did. When somebody drops a sinecure in your lap, you don't turn it down. It keeps me fed and drunk, but of course it also keeps me in Ocotillo. The land that God forgot. But what about you?"

It went against habit for Shoumacher to reveal anything of himself. He shrugged it off. "Fate deals strangely with some of us." A new thought had slipped into his mind, and he was worrying it around, like a dog with a bone.

Dinwiddie said, "Do I detect a gleam of devilment?"

"Something you said," Shoumacher muttered.

"What?"

"Subtlety. A way to knock Farris off his goddam pedestal."

"Why do you hate him so much?"

"Instinct. Chemistry. Who knows? I hate all violent men, especially the ones who find high-sounding excuses for being violent."

"Maybe it's justified."

"Physical violence is never just. It negates everything we—"

"Don't speechify," Dinwiddie said. "I asked you why you hate him, not why you tell your readers to hate him."

"It's the same."

"The hell. Someplace back along the line somebody pushed your head into manure and held you under so long that you never got the stink out of your nose. Somebody a lot bigger and stronger than you. Somebody like Farris. Am I warm?"

"You are impertinent," said Shoumacher, "and presumptuous."

"Uh-huh. I know."

Shoumacher said, "The minute a man straps on a gun, he wipes out a thousand years. It doesn't matter what my private grievances are—I've got a just case against Rand. He ought to be removed. He's a blight on us all."

"He keeps the peace, if you admire that sort of thing."

"Peace?"

"Dead men don't make trouble," Dinwiddie said. He stabbed the scratch pad with his finger. "Anyway, you'll never turn the town against him by writing this kind of stuff."

"Maybe." Shoumacher's eyes came up, popped out. "I'm going to serve him crow for his supper."

"How?"

"He'll hang himself on his own rope."

"And you expect to pull this off all by yourself?"

"Horatius defended the bridge of Rome with just two friends."

Dinwiddie said, "I'm afraid you'll have to talk slower than that, for the benefit of us country boys."

It occurred to Shoumacher that if Dinwiddie had a first name, he had never heard it. He was just drunk enough to pursue that curiosity for a moment before he answered: "This fine, upstanding community has spent quite a time upholding its sense of dignity like a protective cloak over young Clay Rand's head."

"Very literary. But what's it mean?"

"Nobody's ever had the courage to tell Clay about his father's love affairs. Not a word of Rand's peccadillos has reached the lad's tender ears."

"Oh, no," Dinwiddie said quickly. "Phil, certain stones are better left unturned. Believe me."

"Don't spook," Shoumacher said. He looked cross and sulky. "Of course, I need more than that. But a man like Rand just has to have skeletons in his closet. Maybe one of them can toss me a bone. I think I'll send a wire or two and see what I can dig up about his past."

Dinwiddie said, "You have a dangerous mean streak, haven't you? I'd hate to run afoul of it."

"So the sheriff is about to discover."

"Look, let's say you do spill the beans to young Clay. Suppose you even manage to turn him against his father. How in hell does that remove Farris from office?"

Shoumacher rubbed his eyes. "Once you put things into motion, they must follow their course to the end. And half the fun, you know, is in watching the unexpected happen before your eyes. Once you put a burr under someone's saddle, you don't have any idea which way the horse will jump, but you can be damn sure he's going to buck."

"Suppose he lands square on you, with all four hoofs?"

Shoumacher laughed. "You know," he added, "I think we ought to have a talk with McAffee."

"At this hour?"

"He never climbs out of his bottle before dawn."

Dinwiddie said, "All right, hell, why not?" He got up from the table. "But I have a sinking feeling about this. I really do."

Chapter 9

FARRIS Rand stood in the foyer Sunday morning until he heard Clay shut the picket gate. Then he went into the big parlor and strode back and forth, stripped down to his shirtsleeves. He opened the glass jar on the table, selected a cigar and examined it.

His wife came in, tarried for a critical look into the hall mirror, and sat down, wearing a robe over her nightdress. She had a chiseled face, proud and alert; the skin was pulled taut across the high bones. She had brought last evening's newspaper with her like a mute accusation; she folded it back and pretended to read it.

When she glanced up, he was watching her with wry amusement. She laid the newspaper aside. "Where is he going?"

"To his ranch, I imagine. He has a herd of cattle to look after."

"He never tells me anything nowadays."

He said, "I got the impression he was hungry for somebody to talk to. Last night he blew his top at me."

Blue cigar smoke clouded his bold face; his boots tramped a regular oval along the carpet. The head of a twelve-point buck loomed above the fireplace; its wide round eyes stared down on the room. Hanging from one antler was a human scalp.

The furniture was tough and massive, hewn of hard wood and upholstered in leather. Whale lamps threw a yellowed hue against the paneled walls, for it was just on sunrise. In a glass and maple cabinet hung a brace of target pistols and half a dozen rifles and shotguns. Bird guns—the sheriff kept his working arsenal in his courthouse office.

He stopped by the cabinet and took down a .38-56 sporting rifle. With the absent air of a man deep in thought, he began to rub the breech with an oil-brown cloth.

His wife's voice drew his attention. "We are two people afraid of talking to each other, afraid of what they might say. So they don't talk at all."

He took the cigar from his mouth. It had gone out. He put it back in his mouth and touched a match to it.

She said, "Farris, what do I mean to you?"

Taken aback, he masked his momentary confusion by studying his cigar.

"We had love once," she said, "didn't we?"

"I suppose we did."

"What happened to it? Where did it go?"

"Don't you know?"

Her lips pressed together. She turned to the newspaper, but after a moment she began to talk softly of times long ago. He went through the motions of listening, but the bitter mask of his face showed the deceit of it. She cut off her discourse and sat silent until, when he did not leave the room, she said in a cool voice, "Aren't you going to work?"

"I guess so."

"Did you want to talk about something?"

"Maybe. I don't remember. Getting old, I guess." He moved past the oak table and threw open the window; he took down his cigar, holding it in one hand with the rifle, which he had evidently forgotten. He breathed deeply, looking out. The dawn swept in, paling the lamps. He said, "Cold. It's always cold nowadays."

She said, "You've become just as vicious as the worst of them, haven't you?"

"What if I have? How long do you think I'd last if I didn't keep proving that?"

"Proving it to them or to yourself?" Her fingers tapped the folded newspaper.

"No," he said. "I have not read his outburst, and I don't intend to. The writing on outhouse walls is a cut above his stripe."

She said, "Even a liar sometimes tells the truth."

He showed his teeth around his cigar. "This country's been

paid for at the rate of about one dead man for every half mile. Shoumacher will never understand that. He'll be all right thirty years from now, when all this is settled down. But right now he doesn't know how to handle it, and his only answer is to yell. He needs a mouthful of lye soap."

"You commit the sin of intolerance, Farris."

"Among many others, I'm sure."

"You stand on this town like a crowing cock on a dunghill. You have a virtuous self-righteous look of pride like a fortress. I suppose it's never occurred to you that you could be wrong."

"Now and then it does," he said. "I was wrong about Ben Harmony, wasn't I?"

"Yes."

Her eyes, pale blue and stubborn, followed him around the room. She said, "What do you intend doing about Ben?"

"Nothing. It's too late." He seemed to realize he was holding the rifle. He took it back and stood it in its place and wiped the oiled rag along the polished dark wood of the cabinet.

She said, "You have no right to ignore him."

"You sound like Shoumacher. I have every right, and Ben knows that."

"I don't suppose you've even so much as asked him what he wants."

"I know what he wants. He can't have it, and he knows he can't have it. As soon as he's digested that, he'll pull up stakes and move on."

She said, "You're so full of petty wisdom, aren't you?"

"Susan, it was a lot of miles ago."

"Is there a statute of limitations on love?" She stared at him. "I don't understand it. Through some miracle Ben Harmony has grown up decent and intelligent and good. You ought to be grateful. Isn't it enough that you've made him suffer for twenty years?"

His jaw muscles bulged like cables. "He was born to suffer. There's nothing I can do about it."

"If you don't reach out a hand to him, Farris, I swear to you I'll—"

"Don't say anything you'll regret. Just remember this. Ben made up his own mind—I didn't twist his arm. He could have ruined me in this town, but he hasn't."

"And why hasn't he?"

"I don't know."

"Are you that blind?"

"Blind to what?" His eyelids dropped, covering his thoughts. He tossed his cigar on the irons in the fireplace.

Susan sucked in her breath. "Have you ever given him anything except the back of your hand?"

He wheeled. "You've got that stupid, stubborn look on your face. There's no point talking about it."

The distance between them became stuffed with a padded silence; the greatest distances in the world are the distances that separate two people. Finally Susan said, "What kind of world do you think we'd have if everyone were created in your image?"

There was a slow curl of smoke rising from the cigar he had thrown in the fireplace.

She said, "What will happen if Clay finds out about Ben Harmony?"

"I hope, for his sake, he doesn't find out."

"It will be a miracle if he doesn't. You should have told him—a long time ago. Now you'll lose him, and you'll hate yourself for it."

She left her chair. "I've got to dress for church." And she went upstairs.

Susan Rand had an enduring sculptured beauty that did not fade. It was not a deliberate effect; she devoted little time to her toilet. It was true she wore stays; she did not need them; they were the fashion.

She dressed with care, for she would have to represent the family. Her husband ordinarily attended services during the month or two before elections, but this year with the election four weeks away he was running unopposed and probably would make only a token appearance in church the Sunday before Election Day. He disliked the preacher intensely.

Her son, she reflected, had not been to church since last Christmas.

She took a moment to select a dress and bonnet; she was lacing herself into the bodice when she heard the sheriff's knock. When he entered, the first thing he said was, "I don't think we've finished."

"No."

"You look tired."

"I didn't sleep last night. My feet are like ice."

"Feldman's dry goods has some new rubber hot-water bottles."

"Perhaps I'll buy one tomorrow." She sat at the vanity to comb her hair. She could see him in the mirror, critically watching her. He was wearing the gun with the weighted handle. She pulled her eyes away and drew the comb through her hair with long, smooth strokes.

He said, "About Clay."

"Yes?"

"We had a bargain between us. You do know why I had to break it."

"I've heard your—"

"Let me finish. I broke the bargain. I had to. He'd been smothered too long. I couldn't see him fritter his life away on a mediocre musical talent or any of the other notions you had him set on—not after it became clear he wasn't committed to any of them. All right, then. Maybe I lost the boy a long time ago because you forced me to abdicate my place. But —"

"You brought that on yourself."

"No. You pushed me to the wall and used the boy to extort my promise to keep my hands off him. But it doesn't matter now, because he's grown up and he's out of your reach as much as he's out of mine. I just don't want you to make the stupid mistake of thinking you can get him back by filling his head full of stories about Ben Harmony. You might well turn him against me, but he'll never come back to you."

"You really think I'd do that," she said.

"I do."

"We have a rather low opinion of each other, don't we?"

He said, "I know my faults. I'm an arrogant man and sometimes cruel. I have been a poor husband to you and a poor father to Clay. But I've done what I could. I've done what I had to do."

"Yes," she said with a bleak mock-smile. "For example, last night you did what you 'had' to do. You didn't come home until three o'clock this morning."

"Didn't I?"

"You were with one of those women," she said, and closed her eyes.

"Women?"

"All right, then. Whores."

When she looked again in the mirror, he was facing her, laughing softly. He said, "The only distinction I can make is between honest women and dishonest women. Don't talk to me about whores."

It was not the answer she had expected. She gathered herself, as if to leap up. "You don't deny it."

"Would you believe me if I did?"

"I suppose not."

"Well, then," he said.

It was not working out the way she had planned as she lay in bed all through the night listening to insects and occasional passersby on horseback and the distant revelry of the Saturday-night town, and listening for his step on the stairs. She tried to remember the phrases she had composed.

"Mrs. Littlejack puts on a crooked smile whenever she sees me. And Dinwiddie's wife has a special look she saves for me—'Oh, the poor dear, I wonder if she knows'—and—oh, never mind. You've become careless, Farris. You've been changing women the way a penny goes from hand to hand, and everyone in town knows about it."

He was at the window; his profile was inflexible. The cool, precise voice rolled out of his deep chest. "What did you expect of me? You locked me out, knowing that I'm a man, needing what every man needs."

"You want everything on your own terms, don't you?"

"What other terms are there?"

She put down her comb, drew in a deep breath, stood up. "I have never spoken to you of this before."

"And if you're wise you'll never speak of it again."

"If I've kept quiet," she said, "it was for Clay's sake, not mine—not yours."

"Of course," he said. His voice was edged with sarcasm. "Let's be honest, Susan. You don't care how I behave. You only care when people find out about it."

But she had withdrawn; her expression was remote. She tied her bonnet down and gathered her handbag and parasol. "I have pride, too," was all she said.

"You're a fraud," he told her.

"No. I've hated what you've done to me, ever since the first time I saw you hand a fistful of money to that shabby woman in St. Louis."

"You haven't brought that up for twenty years. Now you throw it back in my face again. That night ended it for me. I told you that."

"That night will never end," she said. "It's followed us all these years. Just look in Ben Harmony's face, Farris."

His face closed up. "Go to church. You'll be late."

"Do you think I'll find an answer there?"

"Maybe. You won't find it here. Stop looking back, Susan. The past has no answers for us."

"Then what are we going to do?" she said softly.

His shoulders stirred. "I'm a sheriff, not an oracle."

She stopped at the door, thinking of something to say, but finally she went on without speaking, walked downstairs and left the house.

Chapter 10

OCTOBER in the high country was always unpredictable. Eastern newspapers pictured Arizona as the American Sahara, and presumably readers believed what the newspapers told them, but the fact was that it was nothing of the kind. Scattered across the Territory were patches of arid plain, cluttered with cactus and brush, and the Sonora Desert in the southwest corner was deadly enough, but one-third of the Territory stood upended in immense mountain ranges, many of them heavily timbered and some of them wigged by perpetual snow cover. The other third of Arizona was the great plateaus and basins—vast undulations of grass, aspen groves, juniper, and fir.

The prevailing winds were westerly but had a tendency to shift abruptly from southwest to northwest and back. And the air was bone-dry, possessing no moisture that might store heat. It was not uncommon for the afternoon temperature to reach eighty-five degrees in October and for it to plummet fifty degrees by midnight.

That Sunday morning broke cold and bitter with a slicing wind. With his mackinaw collar turned up around his face, Clay rode his horse up from the creek and squinted into the distance, where a black rug of heavy cloud unrolled toward the basin, shooting dark lances ahead from its crest. He could see the slanted gray streaks of falling rain over the slate-colored mountains far to the west.

He found Ben Harmony lying on the grass, hands behind his head, looking at the clouds as though they were printed poems he could read. A cigarette drooped from the corner of his mouth, and smoke trailed from his nostrils.

A restless uncertainty flooded Clay's features. He exploded into talk.

"Is this all you want, just drifting like a broken-down tramp?"

Ben Harmony murmured, "I get by." He rolled onto one hip and propped his head up on his left hand.

Clay dismounted and let the horse crop grass. He said, "Just getting by isn't good enough for me, I can tell you that. I'm going to put my mark on a piece of this world."

"No point hiding your light under a bushel," Ben agreed.

"It's a me-first country. I figure to take my share."

"Belligerent as hell this morning, ain't you? How's that hangover?"

"I'm all right," Clay lied.

"You're a little nervous."

"I am?"

"Uh-huh. Like something you just rescued from a burning stable."

"Aagh," Clay said in disgust. He turned his back on Ben Harmony, tossing the stirrup over the saddle and fiddling with the cinch buckle. He glanced past the horse at the sky. A misty mother-of-pearl light covered the earth and made him feel the chill.

He said, "Why don't you get a job?"

"For slave wages?"

"How about working for me?"

"Where'd this sudden ambition come from, Chico?"

Clay left the horse. He sat down cross-legged, uprooted a stalk of grass and broke little bits of it. "I want to get married."

Ben Harmony laughed at him. Clay felt his neck warm. He said, "She's soft as syrup, Ben. She has the sparkle of good champagne."

"Sure enough?"

"Did you ever have to sneeze when you had a brim-full cup of coffee in your hands? That's how I feel around her."

"Yeah?" Ben said skeptically. "Looks like you're getting into water above your head, don't it? Maybe you ought to step a ways toward shore."

"Haven't you ever been in love?"

"I've been falling in love since I was fifteen." Ben Harmony twisted the cigarette until it came unstuck from his lip. "No reason to charge head-first into the valley of matrimony."

Clay brooded. Ben Harmony said, "I'm just too curious about the next woman I'm going to meet. Besides, I never did understand the kind of woman who'd rather make one man miserable than a lot of men happy."

"You're a Philistine."

"I had a girl once."

"And?"

"When I was up in Colorado prospecting, I sent my pokes home to her to keep for me. Got back home and found out she'd left town. With her new boyfriend and my money."

"Ooot," said Clay.

"Women are like hats, Chico. If you happen to leave one behind, she's likely not to be there when you go back for her."

"Lavender's not like that."

Ben Harmony waggled a hand. "I was just joshing you. Nobody's easier to fire up than a fellow who thinks he's in love." His casual glance came around. "You asked her yet?"

"Last night."

"She said yes? Then what makes your face so long?"

Clay only shook his head.

"Don't you want to talk about it, Chico?"

"I don't mind."

"But not with me." Ben Harmony's eyes squinted up. "Complications, maybe. The family? Anything to do with me, Chico? I want to know."

Clay said, "Why should it have anything to do with you? You're too damned conceited."

"And you're a bad liar. I guess the young lady's folks don't approve of the company you keep. That it?"

Clay climbed to his feet and hurled the cut-up pieces of grass away violently. "For God's sake." Then his face contorted, and he curled around, twisting his arm with great energy.

"What's the matter?"

"Goddam charley horse in my arm," Clay said. He shook his arm loosely, making faces. "You." He went to his horse. "What makes you think you're at the center of everything?

Can't anybody have troubles without you being convinced you're part of it?"

"If I was wrong," Ben Harmony said, "then forget it."

Clay got mounted and adjusted his boots in the stirrups. He tugged his hat down. "Like I said before, do you want a job?"

"Pushing these cows?"

"I need help building a cabin."

Ben Harmony laughed again. "You're in a hell of a hurry, aren't you?" He uncoiled his long legs and got up. "I hope you and that girl will never be unhappy, Chico."

"Thanks."

"I'll hang around and help out if it won't get you in trouble."

"It won't," Clay said.

Ben Harmony studied him and turned briskly. "Now, where in hell did that cantankerous horse of mine wander off to?"

The Metropolitan Dance Hall (Honest Tables—Dance 5¢—Finest Whiskey) was the last stop on Sheriff Rand's first rounds of the day. Just at noon he stepped out of the place and walked across Holliday Street with his head down in thought.

Billy Cordell caught up to him at the corner of the block. "Howdy."

"Billy."

"I been in eight saloons," Billy Cordell said, "and I put dents in every one of them."

"So I hear. Take care, Billy, or I'll have to run you in."

"Hell, I done no grief. Not yet, anyway. Farris, you look like you got a burden."

"Nothing to trouble you, old friend."

Billy Cordell nodded soberly and flipped his thumb toward the far side of the intersection. "Take a look at who just come crawling out."

The sheriff looked over his shoulder. Deke Stovall was in the mouth of the livery stable, leading his horse. "I posted him out of town last night," the sheriff muttered, and swung off the walk with long strides. Billy Cordell hurried beside him.

Stovall saw them coming. He dropped the reins and

nodded with an expression of pained resignation; he held up his hand, palm out. "All right—all right."

Stovall was wearing a belted revolver, a Colt .45 with a walnut handle. He said, "I'm gettin'."

Billy Cordell said, "The smaller the man, the bigger the gun. Ever notice that?"

Stovall's lip curled back. "I take nothing from you, Billy."

It called forth Billy Cordell's aggressiveness—a quality that never descended far beneath the surface. He said in a very quiet way, "We're about to have us a little fox hunt, Deke. You're the fox." Dropping to a crouch, he flipped up his toad-sticker.

Farris Rand said, "Use that on your fingernails, Billy." He took a pace forward, placing himself between the two men. "Put it in the saddle, Deke. Now."

"You got no authority to post me out of town. I ain't committed no crime." But Stovall's eyes wandered past the sheriff's elbow to the knife in Billy Cordell's blue-veined fist. Clearly Stovall's life was on the tip of Billy Cordell's blade, and Billy Cordell was drunk, and there wasn't a man in Mogollon County who didn't know enough to walk wide around Billy Cordell when he was drunk. Deke Stovall twisted the stirrup, hopped around on one foot until he got himself ready, and hoisted his gaunt, undersized body up on the horse.

With what dignity he could muster, Stovall guided his mount into the street and turned toward the coach road. I'll be seeing you," he said.

"Better not," the sheriff advised.

Billy Cordell's fingers snapped up a rock. He grinned and whooped and threw the rock. It struck Stovall's horse in the flank: the horse spooked, jumped two feet sideways, and broke into a dead gallop. The diminutive rider clung desperately with his seat incongruously balanced across the saddle cantle. The horse spewed back dust, and a startled pedestrian flung himself out of the way. Billy Cordell's hoots of laughter, half roar and half cackle, sang out boldly.

Stovall disappeared around the bend, and the sheriff wheeled wickedly on Billy Cordell. "Give me that thing."

"Hey, we're friends, Farris—remember?"

"I remember. But the next time you pull a knife around me, one of us could be a dead friend. Now give it here."

"Jesus," Billy Cordell said, "if you ain't the goddam toughest nut in the forest!" He thrust his scowling face up against the sheriff's. "Laugh, Farris."

"What for?"

"No reason. Hell, think about Deke. Just laugh."

"Aagh," the sheriff said in disgust.

"You don't know how anymore, do you?" Billy Cordell shook his head. He reversed the knife in his grip, slapped it hilt-first into the sheriff's palm, and walked away with his face gone dull and sad.

Ten feet away he stopped and looked back. "Hey, Farris."

"Yes?"

"Keep your powder dry," Billy Cordell said, and went on his way, bowlegged and old but very definitely unvanquished.

The sheriff's face was as leaden as the building sky. He walked back across the street, chewing his lip, and almost knocked over a pedestrian.

He looked up, glimpsing a woman's skirt, and began to lift his hat. "Sorry, ma'am, I didn't—" He cut it off abruptly when his eyes reached her face. "Hello, Hannah."

Hannah Early inclined her head courteously.

The sheriff's shoulders stirred sluggishly, as if he had rheumatism. Standing in pools of shadow, they regarded each other cautiously.

She said, "How nice to see you," in a synthetic voice.

He nodded and began to turn away. She uttered a sound. He stopped and said, "Yes? What can I do for you that hasn't already been done?"

"You said that a bit too loud, didn't you?"

"What do you want?" he said.

"What do you think?"

It made him grimace. "Don't tell me you start breathing hard whenever I come in sight."

She said, "Hardly. But you been fooling with some ladies you shouldn't be fooling with."

"That's—"

"None of my goddam business, I know. You love your wife, *but.*"

His silence argued with her.

"She doesn't understand you."

"No."

"All right. But think about it—for what you receive, Sheriff, may you be truly thankful."

He said, "What the hell are you talking about now?"

"Just tellin' you to watch your backtrail, that's all. You've gotten too damned careless." Skirts lifted, she went on across the intersection, buttocks writhing, breasts freewheeling. Two of the town's few sober and industrious citizens averted their faces.

The thin lips pursed under the sheriff's silver moustache. One eyebrow made a slight arch. He watched Hannah until she turned the corner and went out of sight.

Chapter 11

CLYDE Littlejack waddled into the office of the *Enterprise* with a conspiratorial over-the-shoulder glance. He swept the pressroom with suspicious scrutiny. Shoumacher watched him patiently.

Satisfied that there were no eavesdroppers, Littlejack finally spoke in a hoarse whisper. "He's sober."

"Think of that. The way you came in here, I thought you were going to tell me there'd been a declaration of war."

Littlejack flushed. Scarlet flowed through his vast cheeks. "I sent Dinwiddie up to his office to keep him company so he won't get drunk right away."

"Then why so secretive, Clyde? If Dinwiddie knows, the whole town will know in a few hours."

"Yeah, I guess that's right."

Shoumacher stripped off his inky apron, reached for his bowler, and went to the coat rack. Littlejack said, "I been reading the paper all week."

"Are your lips tired?"

Littlejack ignored the insult; he probably didn't understand it. He said, "And I ain't seen a thing against Rand all week. How come you've been laying off him?"

"It's a new strategy."

"Uh-huh," Littlejack said, as if he knew what Shoumacher meant.

"The paper hasn't said anything against the sheriff, but it hasn't said anything in his favor, either. In fact, you may have noticed that it hasn't mentioned his name at all."

Littlejack screwed up his face to think about that.

Shoumacher said, "On the other hand, you may have noticed that Colonel McAffee's name has appeared on every page, in practically every column."

"Yeah, I seen that. How come?"

A cutting remark rose to the editor's lips, but died stillborn. He wasn't sure how far he could push Littlejack without offending him. Littlejack was big and slow and warmhearted, like a St. Bernard, but he had a considerable capacity for anger, and when it was fired up, he had all the momentum of a ten-wheel locomotive—he was hard to stop. Shoumacher's dislike of him was compounded of one part contempt and one part physical fear. Littlejack was like a trained bear; Shoumacher was never quite sure when the blacksmith might fly off in an angry, unexpected rage.

He took Littlejack in tow and went outside. A chilly wind swept down the street. The sky was crystalline. Not a cloud anywhere, but the air had a taut feel; it was certain first snow would come early this year. A big hay wagon wended past the courthouse; Shoumacher and Littlejack went up the side stairs into the small dark hall that led to Colonel McAffee's office. McAffee had no official status, but the county provided him with office space, perhaps because he defended most of the cases that came before the courts (not that there were very many cases), or perhaps because he had designed the building and the county felt he had to suffer the consequences.

The colonel was prepared for siege: bulwarked behind his heavy desk, surrounded by bookshelves laden with legal texts, provisioned with a drawer full of John Vale sour mash. Dinwiddie occupied a chair under the window; he scowled when Shoumacher entered. Dinwiddie was probably unhappy because he had failed to keep the colonel from opening his first bottle of the day.

Littlejack shut the door and braced his back against it, as if to prevent an invasion.

Shoumacher said, "You're going to have to go on a strict ration of that stuff, Colonel."

"By whose authority, sir?"

"The voters are not prepared to elect a rumpot to office," Shoumacher said bluntly. "Even I can't put that much across."

"My personal habits are my own concern, I should think."

"You should think," Shoumacher said, "but evidently you don't." He glanced at Dinwiddie for support, and Dinwiddie nodded unhappily.

Littlejack said, "He's right, Colonel. Ain't nobody going to pay much attention if you ain't sober enough to give a few rousing speeches."

"I have never been too drunk to make a speech," McAffee said. He did not regard the statement as funny, but nonetheless Dinwiddie almost fell out of his chair.

Shoumacher's bulging eyes were paler than their surroundings. He took down a Blackstone from the bookcase and pretended to examine it. The act afforded him reason to remain on his feet—a superior attitude that gave him the edge in the conversation. Dinwiddie wiped his eyes with a handkerchief; Littlejack folded his arms across his enormous chest and tucked his chin down, preparing to do his all-out best to follow the subtleties of whatever discussion was to follow.

Shoumacher took the lead. "We have just four weeks to launch a full-bodied campaign that will depose Farris Rand. That's not much time. We've got to—"

Clyde Littlejack said, "Ain't going to be easy knocking Farris down, you know."

Shoumacher turned irritably. "He puts his pants on the same way you do. Don't let him frighten you. Just do your job."

"What job?"

"I'll come to that."

McAffee's hand was on the desk. In the circle of his grip was the bottle of John Vale. He was turning it slowly, pretending to examine the label. He said, "Mr. Shoumacher, let me say I don't much like the way you're acting."

"How so?"

"As if you were in command." The colonel's eyes whipped up, as if to catch Shoumacher off guard and see if he had scored a point.

"I don't like the way you do things," McAffee said. "Made that plain to you before, I think. Don't believe I want you to manage my campaign, if that's what you've got in mind."

"We're on the same side, Colonel."

"Strange bedfellows, then. No secret I've always regarded you as a slimy sort of creature."

Shoumacher contained his irritation. "Colonel, if we want to knock Rand off his perch and replace him with you, then you and I have got to make peace between us."

"You're asking a lot of a good hater," McAffee said.

Shoumacher put the book back in place on the shelf and slammed it home. "All right. Now you listen to me, Colonel, because I want this settled right now. Ever since you came to this town you've wanted political office. You ran for county judge. And lost. You ran for mayor. And lost. Now you want to run for sheriff. You're getting a very late start in the race, and you haven't got so many friends that you can afford to be too particular about pedigree. Let me make it clear to you—I can put you in office. Without me, you're holding a bust hand. Now, sometimes you're a little hasty in what you consider to be your judgments. You put on a fine show of indignation when the spirit moves you, but you and I both know that you'd set fire to your own mother if you could get a good price for the ashes. So let's not fence with each other."

McAffee murmured, "You're getting to a point, sir. What is it?"

"I think I've just made it."

"No. You've made noise. You haven't told me why you want to help me or how you can deliver the office to me. Or have you got an exaggerated picture of the influence you wield with that yellow rag you print?"

Dinwiddie crossed his legs and steepled his fingers. His stovepipe hat stood on the windowsill beside him. He said, "Gentlemen, gentlemen. Must we destroy each other's dignity before we get down to cases? Phil, there's no need to insult the colonel. And vice versa."

Shoumacher flashed a bug-eyed, petulant look at him, but then he realized Dinwiddie was right. About the only virtue the colonel had left was his sense of dignity, and it might not serve their best interests to prick that.

He said in a tone meant to placate, "It may be that my newspaper is not held in biblical esteem. But people do read it. They may ignore the editorials, but they read the news. They believe facts when the facts are brought to their attention. And all I need to do to slip you into the sheriff's office is give the people a few facts to chew on."

"What facts?" McAffee said.

"Information concerning Farris Rand."

"What kind of information?"

"Documentation of certain affairs in his past," Shoumacher purred, "which, not to put too fine a point on it, could be described as questionable."

"Name them."

"Not yet," Shoumacher said. "I've wired some people in the Midwest. The information is still coming in. I'm not yet at liberty to—"

"Goddam it," the colonel roared, "you haven't said a thing."

"I'll say this," Shoumacher answered. "The facts I'll print will make Rand's position untenable. And all of us know that voters are a crochety breed. They vote against, not for. They'll vote against Rand."

"And, therefore, *for* you," said Dinwiddie.

"By default," the colonel grumbled. "Hell of a way to win an election."

"Don't be such a farmer," Shoumacher said. "Are you afraid to gamble? Colonel, everybody who comes West comes to gamble. What have you to lose?"

"On the contrary," McAffee said. "The question is, what have you to gain?"

"What difference does that make?"

"It could make a great deal. You hate Rand, don't you? Why?"

"I don't know why. And I don't care enough to find out. What does it matter?"

"At least Farris Rand is a man," McAffee said. "You're only a bad joke, Shoumacher."

Shoumacher's eyes seemed ready to pop out of the sockets. He said grimly, "Colonel, I'm bending over backwards to help you. Now if you don't—"

"You're bending over backwards so far that you're standing on your head," McAffee said.

Dinwiddie sat up. "Gents, for Christ's sake, simmer down. Look, Colonel, just tell me this. What lengths would you go to to get elected?"

"Whatever lengths I might have to go to."

"Then what are you arguing about?"

"A man likes to know who his friends are."

Dinwiddie said, "You've got a lot more sand than I gave

you credit for, I'll say that." He laughed. "You know, I'll bet you wouldn't make such a bad sheriff, at that."

The colonel swelled up. "Thought I was a joke, did you? Thought I'd be a willing puppet. I'll warn all three of you—if I'm elected, I intend to be my own man."

"Sure you do," Shoumacher said. "Look, we don't care about that right now."

"I think you do," McAffee said. "If you didn't, we wouldn't be having this conversation."

Shoumacher said, "Let's win the election first."

Clyde Littlejack said, "That ain't going to be too hard, the way Farris has been coddling that nigger. First he hangs a no-trespassin' sign on him, and the next thing you know the nigger's took over that ranch of Clay's and running it like it was his own."

"You don't need to tell me about that Nigra," said McAffee self-righteously. "Shiftless no-good if I ever saw one. Came into town on a horse that's got at least nine brands on it."

Dinwiddie said, "Maybe that just shows there were a lot of unsatisfied horse-buyers. Are you trying to make him out a thief?"

"That Nigra insulted me, sir," said McAffee. "On the street in broad daylight."

"He seems to have insulted everyone in town," Shoumacher observed.

"He's not what you'd call retiring," said Dinwiddie.

McAffee said, "I told him then, and I'll tell you now, that Nigra hasn't been in this town long enough to talk to a white man like that."

"How long does it take?" Dinwiddie asked insinuatingly.

"What?"

Dinwiddie passed it off with a hand wave. "Never mind. The fact is, for some reason of his own, Farris has gone out on a limb to look out for the colored boy—maybe because he's a friend of Clay's. Anyhow it's stirred up a lot of people. Folks don't like it."

"As far as we're concerned," Shoumacher said, "it couldn't have happened at a better time."

Clyde Littlejack said, "Farris ain't the kind you can cotton up to close, but I used to respect him. But I got no use for nigger lovers. He done lost my vote. I don't mind telling you

I can't figure it. Seems like he's just forgot his place, Farris has. I mean, we got plenty nigger cowhands around the valley, but he never took up for none of them before."

McAffee said, "None of them ever overstepped the bounds before. They know their place, even if the sheriff doesn't."

"The ex-sheriff, let's call him," Shoumacher said with a dry smile.

Chapter 12

THE sheriff's wife turned into the alley, studied the buildings curiously, and selected a door. She went up the steps, holding up her skirts, and knocked firmly.

Hannah Early answered the door. "Good evening." If she was surprised, she didn't show it.

Susan Rand looked her up and down with distaste. It made Hannah grin with one side of her mouth. "Looks like you ain't pleased."

"May I come in?"

"It'd be better if you didn't. You know that."

"Do you mind terribly if I insist?" It was evident she was holding things precariously in check.

Hannah stepped aside, admitted her, and closed the door. It was stuffy in the foyer; the little buffer room was bare of furnishings except for a wall lamp. Susan Rand said, "What an ugly place."

"Don't let it fool you. I got a full jewel box."

"Of course," Susan Rand said. "The spoils of war. Or is it love? I always confuse the two."

"Some women got a talent for turning one into the other," said Hannah.

"How kind of you to remind me." Susan Rand's voice ran along the correct scale of mock courtesy, but the fear and rage behind it made it quiver, off-key.

Hannah said, "All right, Mrs. Rand. You don't approve of me, which is as it should be, I guess. Let's get to the point."

Susan Rand looked her in the eye. "Is that all you have to say to me?"

"What do you want me to say?"

The sheriff's wife maintained her self-possession with an obvious effort. "All right. Since you evidently enjoy forcing me to ask, I shall. I expect to find my husband here."

"Do you?" Hannah said. With sudden temper she added, "And what do you figure he expected to find here that he couldn't find at home, Mrs. Rand?"

"You may as well not waste energy trying to humiliate me. You won't succeed."

Hannah said, "Do you *like* being trampled, Mrs. Rand? Is that why you came here?"

"I'm trying to understand it," Susan Rand answered. She drew a breath. "Is he here? Please, I must know."

Hannah turned without a word, went to a small side door and opened it. A narrow flight of stairs led upward, lit by a single lantern at the top. Susan Rand followed Hannah with slow reluctance. She had a slim, firm body, and a resentful part of her hated having to compete with Hannah's big surging breasts and hips.

They went down a hall. One door stood ajar, and a man's gruff voice could be heard plainly. "Jesus, Minnie, I been three months with those goddam sheep, and I'm ready to spend twenty-four hours and then some. I'd sure like to stoke your furnace some more."

"Cash on the barrel, Johnny. Silver or greenbacks," said a girl with a high-pitched voice.

"Hell, I got a whole pocket full of greenjackets. Right over there in my pants. Count 'em."

Hannah reached the door at the end of the corridor and turned to wait for Susan Rand to come up. The girl's voice said, "Sure enough. But take a bath first, Johnny. You smell like a bag of dirty laundry."

"Anything you say, Minnie darlin'."

"How many sheep have you got, anyway?"

"How 'n hell do I know? 'Fore I finish counting them, I always fall asleep." The man guffawed.

Hannah threw the door open and stood aside. Susan Rand arranged her face and went in.

He was awake. For a moment his eyes observed without believing, and then he gave a bray of laughter. He tossed the bedclothes on the floor and stood up on his feet. Something fixed her eyes on the livid scar along his belly that a Confederate saber had carved. Except for his hands and face, his strong body was as white as the underside of a fish. *It is the first time I have seen him this way in so long that I can't remember*.

His laughter dried up. He kicked the blanket away from his feet and walked to the commode; he bent over to wash his face.

Hannah walked past Susan, reached for a towel and held it out. The sheriff's fumbling grasp found the towel; he muttered something. There was no particular triumph in Hannah's eyes; she watched Susan Rand.

The sheriff rubbed his face dry. "Now. What in hell is the matter with you?"

"I must speak to you. It's important."

"It had better be." He reached for his underclothes. Susan Rand glanced quickly away; she turned her back.

Hannah said, "I think it'd be nice if you cleaned up that mess before you get out of here." She pointed at the bedclothes all over the floor.

He said, "Tell that to your maid, not to me." He walked out of the room without waiting for either of them.

Deliberately Susan Rand bent and picked up the bedclothes, folded them into exact rectangles, and piled them neatly on the bed.

Hannah tilted her face to one side. Susan Rand gave her a bleak glance and walked out, pulling the door shut as she went.

He did not wait. She had to follow him all the way home.

When she entered the house, he had already hung up his hat. He threw off his coat and hurled it toward the divan. It fell off and lay in a heap on the carpet.

She trembled in fury. "Goddam you."

"What do you want?"

"Don't use that tone on me, Farris. Don't you ever use that tone on me."

He snapped, "What do you want?" He walked to the big table and poured a drink, swirled it in the glass and drank it down.

She said, "They're getting married. He says they're going to get married."

He frowned at her. "Who? Make sense."

"Clay. Clay and Lavender."

It brought forth his harsh laugh again. It sounded just the way it had sounded in Hannah Early's bedroom. He said, "And you dragged me home for *that*?"

"Farris, I'm quite serious."

"I can see that," he said, "though I'm damned if I can understand it. What is there about this that wouldn't keep till morning, for God's sake?"

"He plans to announce it in the morning," she said.

"What of it?"

"I couldn't make him promise not to. He only agreed to wait until morning."

"Jesus Christ, Susan, what are you talking about?"

"She's McAffee's granddaughter, Farris. Don't you understand at all?" The evening paper lay on the divan. She tossed it down in front of him. "While you were enjoying yourself, McAffee was making a speech on the courthouse steps. I hadn't stopped to think—I don't suppose you can have heard about it. You'd better read that."

He only glanced at the lead paragraph and laughed again. "The old fool. He'll never surrender, will he?"

"Look at it, Farris. He had half the town out there listening to him."

"What of it? People around here welcome any entertainment. They turned out to hear Eddie Foy, too. It didn't get him elected to office."

"They liked what they heard," she said tightly. "And if it gets into tomorrow's paper that Clay is marrying Stanton McAffee's granddaughter, everyone will take it to mean Clay's turned against you and is supporting McAffee."

"I'm sure Clay has nothing of the kind in mind."

"That's not the point, Farris."

"Then what is the point? Why all this sudden concern for my political welfare?"

"Your welfare be damned," she said. "But I will not have Clay dragged into the middle of a filthy political fight. You've got to talk to him and convince him that he must not announce any wedding plans until after the election."

"I don't see why I should," he said. He seemed amused. "After all, if you want to read politics into it, it just could be that Lavender is throwing the weight of her support behind me, instead of the other way around."

"Don't make a joke out of it. You know perfectly well that nobody will believe anything like that. She's a woman."

"I should hope so."

"Clay knows nothing about this kind of thing. If you let him go ahead, it will be in tomorrow's newspaper, and he'll find himself in an awful situation."

"Did you explain that to him?"

"Yes."

"Then I don't see there's much for me to do, if he's made up his mind."

"You've got to stop him," she said. "I couldn't make him understand."

"I don't wonder. You're not making too much sense."

"His innocence," she said, "has been his best defense. But now—"

"You mean his only defense. And a damned poor one at best."

"He'll be caught up in this thing that's none of his own doing. He'll be right in the middle, by himself."

"He's always been by himself," he said. "At least he's learned to believe in himself and make a decision. It's about time you stopped crying over him. He's turning into a man to be proud of."

He refilled his glass and glanced down at the newspaper. "Shoumacher," he muttered. "A quill pen and a pot of vituperation. That's what you'd have turned Clay into—a waspish bitter little man like Shoumacher. He'd never have fitted in. Not your way. But he's free of both of us now."

He stood by the table, drinking slowly. Only one lamp was lighted, in the front of the room. Farris Rand's head was in shadow; his face was only a dark suggestion. Then he turned so that a little of the lamplight struck his features. His face was marble-colored, no warmer. The moustache drooped across his lips. He said, "If Clay has decided on that, I won't stand in his way."

A long time went by before she spoke. Finally she said, "I have known you to be cruel, but never like this."

"He'll be all right. I'm sure of it."

"It's nice to be sure."

"You've got a sharp tongue."

"Have I?"

He said, "Want to know what I think, Susan? I think what

really bothers you is the possibility that you may not be the wife of the sheriff very much longer. If I were to lose the election, it would take your position in this town down a peg or two, wouldn't it?"

"How can you!"

He studied her over a stretching, broken interval, and finally he said, "I'm sorry, Susan. I think I had that wrong. I apologize."

"You apologize," she said bitterly. "You apologize, and that makes everything right, does it?"

He blinked and lifted his drink. She said, "You'd like to slap me, wouldn't you? You'd like to shout at me and beat me black-and-blue. You never tell me what you're thinking inside that head of yours."

She strayed from the grip of his eyes. "I can't look at you. I hardly recognize you anymore."

He shook his head. "I know I've hurt you."

"You could say you hurt me. You could say that."

He prowled the room until he was within two strides of her. He gripped his drink in both hands. "Do you think I've wanted to be alone, Susan?"

"You've never said a word to make me doubt it."

"It was your choice, not mine."

"Farris, you're a castle without a drawbridge. You're the most distant man I've ever known."

"What makes you think you know me?" he asked.

"There. That's just what I mean." He was standing too near; she crossed the room on the pretext of lighting another lamp.

She said, "I think we've both said too much."

"Uh-huh."

"What's the matter with us? Can't we do anything but quarrel?"

"I apprehend that there've been moments when it might have been different," he said. He sipped his whiskey. "But it's too late now, and it has been altogether too long since you shut your bedroom door against me. I'm a virile man, which is a fact you chose to ignore, and I'm a proud man, which you have pointed out. I will not beg, Susan, and I will never promise to be any different from what I am."

She had a full, clear prescience of what he would say, but

she put it to him. "What you're saying is that no matter what I say or do, you don't intend to give up a thing."

"Neither Hannah Early nor her kind," he said brutally.

It would be difficult, she reflected, to chill the atmosphere between them any further without turning it to solid ice. She answered in kind.

"Be careful what you say to me, Farris, or I'll pack my things and move out of this house. And I am not—"

"Pack."

"What?"

"Pack." He set down his drink and approached the divan to pick up his coat from the floor. "I don't want to find a trace of you here when I get back."

When the sound of his boots was gone, she climbed the stairs slowly. She opened the door to his bedroom and stood on the threshold, but she did not go in. In time she turned down the landing to her own room.

She stared around the room, not knowing where to begin.

She heard him return, a quarter of an hour later. She heard him come upstairs and listened to his boots come forward. When he knocked, she bit her lip and did not answer. He came inside and left the door standing open.

"Do you mind if I come in?"

"I do."

He did not move. He seemed subdued. "I've seen Clay."

"Have you? How nice."

He said, "Look, do you mind if we talk this out?"

"You're still my husband. I suppose that gives you certain rights."

"You look lovely," he told her.

She inclined her head. He said, "Do you know that cold smile doesn't suit you?"

"Get on with it, Farris."

"He's in love with the girl."

"He's nineteen," she said. "He's in love with the idea of being in love."

"No. The way he looks when he talks about her you could pour on a pancake." He smiled slightly. "I wanted him to toughen up. I didn't ever want him to get sentimental. But you can't help seeing his side of it. He's put his whole heart on the line. He's made her the offer of trust."

"All the more reason to convince him he's got to postpone his plans."

"No. If you overprotect something, you lose it. If you'd really looked at his face, instead of your own fear for him, you wouldn't have had to say that."

"Is that what you really believe, Farris, or is it only what you want to believe?"

He lighted his cigar. She turned her back to him, went past the open valise on the bed, and bent forward to look in the mirror. "Just look at my hair." She turned her face from side to side, studying the effect. "Why did you come back here?"

"I think he ought to be spared this."

"This what?"

"You and me. He doesn't need to know about that"—he indicated the half-packed valise—"at least until after he's had a chance to strike his own path. I think it would be a good idea to invite people around to the house one night. Give Clay and his young woman a party."

She suspected him immediately. She said, "That would do nicely, wouldn't it? To convince the town there was no break between you and Clay. To mend your political fences."

"You've been honest with me tonight," he said, "I'll return the favor. That thought was in my head. I'll admit it. We're all sinners, Susan. Born in sin, live and die in sin. But nothing's as simple as we'd like it to be, and I think this would be the best thing for all of us. Particularly our son. I'd like you to be the hostess. Be my wife, just for that day in Clay's life. Next month will be soon enough for him to learn about us."

She fastened her will, like steel hoops, around her feelings. She said, "I'll remind you that you were the one who ordered me out of this house."

"Forget that. Forget that, and stay."

"Tonight, or forever?"

"That's for you to decide."

He turned to the door, carrying his cigar. "I've said what I came to say."

She said, "I don't understand any part of you. You hate the sight of me, don't you?"

"The sight of you," he said gravely, "is just about the only thing I don't hate."

She laughed, with tears close beneath her laughter. "All

right, Farris. But only for Clay. I'll play the dutiful wife—if I can remember the part. I won't deprive Clay of his illusions until after your party—after the election, perhaps. Now get out of my bedroom."

"Thank you," he said. His face betrayed no feelings. He walked out, leaving the door ajar.

Chapter 13

From the window of his father's office Clay could see the lamps come alive along Partridge Street. Scotty's swamper splashed a bucket of water across the welk in front of the Occidental and pushed the suds into the street with a broom. In front of Dunson's Apothecary three farm kids sat on the tailgate of a buckboard, laughing, drinking strawberry phosphate. Things were so simple when you were a kid.

His father looked up from the desk, took the cigar out of his mouth, and said, "When you were in school, you were nothing but a two-legged stack of books. Now you look like a man. It looks like you've cut your eyeteeth. You put yourself up against a grindstone when you started ranching and went on that roundup drive. I was interested to see whether it would grind you down or polish you up. You turned out to be made of pretty hard stuff." Smoke curled around his head, and he batted it away, squinting. "But I notice you haven't spent much time at home. Is that on account of your mother?"

"I don't know. I guess so."

"You're finding it hard to face her. You feel as though she'd turned against you."

"You see a lot, don't you?"

"I've lived long enough to pick up a few pointers," his father said. "But you ought to remember this. What your mother did she did in your own best interests. She wasn't trying to discourage you out of spite."

"Did she ask you to say that?"

"Is that what you think?"

99

Clay said, "She still thinks I'm a kid."

"All mothers are like that."

Clay wiggled his toes inside his boots. Traffic along the street was picking up. He saw Hannah Early walk down the street from the Chinese cafe, wearing a shawl, smiling and joking with the men she passed. Clay said, "I've got a lot of time to make up for."

"How so?"

"I wasted a lot of time on books and piano playing and stuff like that."

"Wasted? What's your hurry, Clay? Where are you off to that you've got to get up a head start?"

"If I'd waited much longer, I'd have been old."

His father laughed at him and said, "I hope that's not the reason you want to marry that girl right away."

"No, sir."

Harry Greiff put his head in the doorway. "Anything you want before I go and eat?"

"No. Go ahead," said the sheriff.

"We ain't heard from the reservation. What do you aim to do about Richardson?"

"Let him go in the morning. We haven't got enough evidence to convict him."

"Yes, sir," said Greiff. He turned to go.

"Mr. Greiff."

"Sir?"

"Make sure he clears out of this jurisdiction."

"Just so," said Harry Greiff, and went.

Clay's father said, "Things are quiet around here. In a way I wish they weren't. People forget damned fast. They think they've got a grudge against me—they've forgotten what this town was like before I came here. They're not so far behind the frontier as they'd like to think. This territory's still hide-out and headquarters for every hooligan from the States. If this place gets soft, the word will go around. McAffee means well, but he doesn't know his ass from a hole in the ground when it comes to law enforcement."

"Uh-huh."

"But that's not your problem, is it?" his father said gently.

Clay was watching the street. He saw Ben Harmony threading the traffic on his disreputable horse. Ben Harmony's collar was turned up; a bit of steam chugged from the horse's nostrils. It was cold out there.

He said, "Think I'll go and eat."

"Why not come home for supper?"

"I've made other plans," said Clay. He left his father at the desk.

Lavender was incarcerated with her seamstress. Clay wasn't sure what to do with himself. He didn't want to go home. He saw Ben Harmony's horse parked in front of the Occidental; he went into the place, met Ben Harmony in the bar, and took the five-cent bar supper with a glass of whiskey. Billy Cordell hung thick over a glass at the end of the bar, looking as if he were ready to pick a fight at the drop of a hat even if he had to drop the hat himself; by way of warning, Scotty had lifted the sawed-off pool cue from behind the bar and laid it in plain sight. Billy Cordell ignored it. At the green felt table Clyde Littlejack was playing cards with Dinwiddie and some others. Dinwiddie looked very professional; he wore a green eye-shade and sleeve garters, celluloid collar and cuffs, but everybody in town knew he was a terrible card player.

Billy Cordell edged toward Clay and Ben Harmony and made desultory conversation. Littlejack squirmed bulkily around in his chair to look at the Negro, baleful and stubborn. Philip Shoumacher came in, hung up his coat by the door, and raked the place with his glance—the hyperthyroid eyes made bumps on his face. At the card table Littlejack said, "Money on wood makes the game go good," and aggressively shoved a bet into the pot.

Billy Cordell took a drink. His calm face was betrayed by bright, reckless eyes. The sheriff appeared in the doorway, looking in on his rounds, and just about then Shoumacher stopped, having spied Billy Cordell. He stood there, frankly watching Billy Cordell, and the sheriff walked in, speaking a few pleasantries to men as he passed. He said to Billy Cordell, "Still drinking the same cheap brand, I see."

Shoumacher said, "You know this man, don't you, Sheriff?"

The sheriff turned. Shoumacher said, "He drove his buckboard into a puddle and soaked my wife with mud. And then he laughed."

Billy Cordell said, "Think you're man enough to do anything about that?"

Shoumacher swallowed. The sheriff said with a dry rustle, "Do you want to swear out a complaint?"

Shoumacher shrugged. "I don't suppose it's worth the trouble. But I must say you make strange friends, Sheriff."

"I see you're in your usual good humor this evening," the sheriff said by way of reply.

By that time Ben Harmony had walked over to the card table. Clay was startled to hear him say, "Mind if I sit in?"

Littlejack snarled. "It's a private game."

Billy Cordell started to grin. The sheriff turned around. Ben Harmony was standing by the table; he had picked up the deck of cards—absently, it seemed—and he said, "What's the matter, Clyde?" The cards riffled and chattered rapidly, expertly, in his hands.

Littlejack said, "Take care the way you run your thumb over that pack, nigger boy."

Ben Harmony tossed the pack down. The cards scattered across the table. His voice hit Littlejack like the flat of a hand. "Maybe you'd like to try saying that again."

Littlejack stirred, ready to rise, but Sheriff Rand's eyes jammed him back down in his seat.

The sheriff said, "Don't get forward, boys. Now let's just back off." His scrutiny shifted shrewdly back and forth from Ben Harmony to Littlejack.

But Littlejack wasn't willing to let it lie. He said, "No telling but maybe some of the lampblack gonna rub off his skin onto them cards, hey, Farris?"

Ben Harmony said, without taking his eyes off Littlejack, "Tell me something, Sheriff. Is it a misdemeanor to lay into somebody as big as Clyde, here? Because in a minute he's going to be picking up his teeth with two busted arms."

Littlejack's lip curled back. "Nigger, you want carvin' up."

Dinwiddie slid his chair back, round-eyed, and Billy Cordell's lips stirred in a private bloodthirsty smile. The sheriff said, "I think both of you had better find yourselves another trough to swill at."

Littlejack gripped the edge of the table. "Farris, this nigger's talking out of turn, and I don't aim to take no more of it. Maybe he's got you and the rest of this town buffaloed, but not me, no, sir. Not me."

Ben Harmony taunted him: "You don't like this?"

Farris Rand said, "Either one of you start anything and I'll shoot your ears off."

Shoumacher showed a sneer of contempt in response to that. He said, "That would be just like—"

"Shut up, Shoumacher. You're out of order." The sheriff did not so much as glance at him. He rested the palm of his hand against the grip of his revolver.

But the slow machinery of Littlejack's temper had been set in motion, brought to its head of steam by a week's grinding resentment. Littlejack's fingers whitened and his shoulders bunched, and as if it were made of papier-mâché, he heaved the table up against Ben Harmony.

The sheriff bellowed. Ben Harmony stumbled, caught amidships by the edge of the table; he flung the table aside and got his balance. Right about then Billy Cordell whooped and, for no ostensible reason, flung the contents of his whiskey glass into the face of Philip Shoumacher. Shoumacher went backward, crying out and pawing at his eyes. Littlejack launched himself forward and hit Ben Harmony in the face; there was a terrible racket when Ben Harmony went down, knocking a chair down with him and sending the upset table skittering away. The sheriff roared and stamped forward, but Ben Harmony dodged around him and swatted Littlejack in the mouth. Billy Cordell's knife was flashing. Clay grabbed him by the arm and yelled in his ear. Ben Harmony aimed a blow into Littlejack's ample belly. Littlejack grunted and settled back on his heels. Clay saw the dark blur of Ben Harmony's fist; it met Littlejack's nose, sounding like an ax against an ironwood tree. Blood spurted across Ben Harmony's knuckles, and Littlejack began to turn a little green.

Billy Cordell spun out of Clay's grasp, clamped a bystander from behind in a bum's-rush grip, and propelled the bystander lustily across the floor, throwing him through the half-doors. Cordell wove a wildly improbable path back into the melée, where the sheriff had stepped between Littlejack and Ben Harmony and was displaying his revolver. The sheriff's face was wickedly enraged. "That is enough!" Clay stepped in to give him support, placing himself face to face with Ben Harmony and pushing Ben Harmony back, palms against shoulders. Ben Harmony's face was scowling, and he was breathing hard.

Clay glimpsed Philip Shoumacher waving his arms impotently, blinded by the whiskey in his eyes. Billy Cordell stumbled by, light racing fragmentarily along the swinging blade of his knife. The knife was arching toward Shoumacher's belly, and Farris Rand snapped: "Billy!" But the knife kept moving. Shoumacher lost his balance and fell down, grinding his knuckles into his eye sockets, and Billy Cordell screeched, pouncing on him.

The sheriff's gun whipped around. "Stop it, Billy." But Billy Cordell did not hear him, and the sheriff leveled his aim.

The shot boomed.

Its concussion knocked out half the lamps in the place. The bullet knocked Billy Cordell's legs out from under him; he spilled onto the floor.

Clay shrank back, seeing Shoumacher scuttle away, still blinded and terrified. The explosion froze Littlejack and Ben Harmony in their tracks.

Billy Cordell rolled over. He seemed confused. "Goddam bastard son-of-a-bitch, what the hell—"

The sheriff said, "Don't be bitter, Billy. Just lie there and shut up."

Billy Cordell said, "I hit somewhere?"

The sheriff glanced at Littlejack, at Ben Harmony, and at Clay. Then he hurried across the room and knelt by Cordell. "In your leg. How does it feel?"

"Startin' to hurt like hell, Farris."

"You're all right, then. The bad ones don't hurt much." He peeled back the pants leg. "As long as you had to get yourself shot, that's as good a place as any for it."

"That's the third time I've took lead in that leg," said Cordell. "Least you could've hit the other one. It's virgin."

Clay stood soaked in his own juices, panting for breath. Shoumacher got up, scraping his eyes. Dinwiddie was still in his chair, gripping the arms and swallowing frantically. Ben Harmony and Littlejack stood silent, not looking at each other.

Billy Cordell said, "What was I doing?"

"You went after Shoumacher with a knife."

"Think of that," said Cordell.

Shoumacher was making inarticulate noises. He had his handkerchief pressed against his face. Billy Cordell looked down with wonder. "Look at me bleed!" Then he grinned at the sheriff. "Thanks for not killing me."

"Go to hell, Billy."

Shoumacher said, "Cordell, you talk as if you had a future. By God, I'm going to throw the whole library at you. You'll hang!"

Cordell looked up at the sheriff. "Christ's sake, Farris, you ain't going to *hang* me."

"I guess not," the sheriff said. He got to his feet and swept the trembling crowd with his eyes. "I think that's all, gentlemen."

The light was eerie, flickering. Shoumacher dusted himself off. "Sheriff, Goddam it—"

"Shut up," Farris Rand said. "Just shut up, will you please?"

Billy Cordell, bloodstained and proud of it, struggled into a sitting position. Scotty came out from behind the bar with a towel, which he used on Cordell's leg. The sheriff's eyes roamed from face to face. Ben Harmony exhaled a blast of wind, and Clay said, "Ben."

"Yeah?"

"You all right?"

"Sure."

"I'm not as young as I was a few minutes ago." He went over to the bar and draped his arms over it; he felt weak behind the knees.

Littlejack's face was rich with blood. He raised a hand to his nose and brought it away, staring at the palm. He began to swear, exploding in a long string of oaths.

The sheriff lifted Billy Cordell to his feet by one arm. "Clyde."

"What?" Littlejack said resentfully.

"Get Dr. Smyley. Tell him to meet us at the jail."

"But I—"

"Move!"

Littlejack mouthed a profane protest. He eyed Ben Harmony, who returned his glance without humor or malice. "Move," the sheriff said again. Littlejack walked reluctantly to the door, looked over his shoulder, and left.

Ben Harmony crossed the floor and got his shoulder under

Billy Cordell's free arm. Clay wiped his mouth nervously and
joined them. The sheriff said, "Come on, Billy."

"Where to?"

"Jail."

"What the hell for? What'd I do?"

"We'll talk about it later."

The crowd opened to let them through.

Emmett Smyley was a frontier sawbones, but nobody ever
called him Doc. He came in with his bag, into Billy Cordell's
cell, and had a look at the bullet wound.

"What a hell of a mess," he said. "You picked a hell of a
place to shoot him, Farris. What a hell of a mess you made."

Billy Cordell said, "What's the matter, Pete's sake?"

"This is a hell of a place to go digging for a bullet. I'm
likely as not to ruin your knee joint. Hell of a thing."

Billy Cordell cackled weakly, "Kind of makes the hill high
to climb, don't it?"

Harry Greiff brought a bottle of whiskey into the cell. Billy
Cordell's eyes lit up. "That for me?"

The doctor said, "Drink as much of it as you can. I want
you out cold."

"Take more'n you can put in a bottle that size," Billy
Cordell said. "Hell, I can put that much in my eye."

"You put enough in Shoumacher's eye," said Farris Rand.
"Try putting this batch down your throat."

The doctor said, "Get the hell out of here, Farris."

The sheriff went back to his office and tossed the keys on
his desk. He regarded Ben Harmony for a long hot moment.
"You've got the courage of your ignorance, that's for sure.
You almost got two men killed. You know that, don't you?"

"Don't try that on me, old man. I'm not Billy Cordell's
keeper."

The sheriff sat down slowly behind the desk, as if his joints
had gone stiff on him. Clay moved over and sat hipshot on
the windowsill, shaking a little all over his body.

The sheriff said, "Pride and dignity and defending yourself
—that's one thing, Ben. But you've been trying to pick a fight
ever since you came here. You won't get old that way, boy."

Ben Harmony was grinding his fist into his palm. The
sheriff said, "It's time you learned that the skill of his fists is
no measure of a man." There were deep lines graven in his

forehead. "I had to shoot a friend of mine tonight to save that fool's life."

"I didn't ask you to thank me," Ben Harmony snapped. "And if Cordell's any example of the friends you pick—"

"He is my friend," the sheriff repeated slowly. "I don't give a damn for your opinion, Ben. Keep it to yourself."

"Sure," Ben Harmony said, sour.

"Now you listen to me," the sheriff said. "The trouble we had tonight was your doing, nobody else's. I'll have no more of it. I want you packed and out of town as fast as you can make it."

Clay came to his feet. "He works for me."

"Then fire him."

"No, sir. Not until I want to."

The sheriff ground his jaws. "Don't fight me on this, Clay. I won't have it."

Clay said, "I go a long way with you, and you know it. But I know about the law, enough to know you can't just throw a man out of town without a hearing or a reason. You did it to Stovall and some others, and maybe there was some justice in that, but Ben didn't start the fight over there and—" His voice petered out.

"And what?"

Ben Harmony said, "You don't have to fight battles for me, Chico. Thanks just the same, but I'll handle my own."

The sheriff said, "There's a thin line between starting a fight and provoking it. Littlejack may have thrown the first blow, but we all know who started it."

A caustic voice said, "I'm glad to hear that." It was Colonel McAffee. He had been standing out in the hall listening; he came in, paunch preceding him like a prow, gesturing with his walking stick. He lowered his head and stared around at each of them from under tufted brows. He stared so long that the sheriff finally said, "Is there something you want to say?"

"Came here to see what kind of justice you'd hand out, not to make a speech."

"That will be the day," the sheriff observed.

"Are you going to jail this black ruffian, sir?"

"I'll give it some thought," the sheriff said.

"If you don't, you'll—"

"I'll what?" the sheriff demanded.

McAffee hiccupped. "You'll no doubt regret it," he purred, smiling synthetically.

"One regret more or less doesn't count for much with me anymore," Farris Rand said. He tipped his head back. "Do you really want this job? You're a fool, Colonel."

McAffee's glance swept past Ben Harmony as if he weren't there. It touched on Clay and settled back on the sheriff. "Heard the Nigra started a free-for-all. I'm surprised he's not locked up. Fair to warn you, if you let him walk the streets after this, you'll lose whatever friends you have left around here. Thought about that, Farris?"

"I did not," the sheriff answered, "and I will not."

McAffee said, "Might be embarrassing if Clyde Littlejack has to swear out a complaint."

"Let him," said Ben Harmony. "I'll file a countercharge."

McAffee gave him a bland, level look. "Boy," he said gently, "you don't think that would get you very far in this town, do you?" He smiled with satisfaction.

"It will," Farris Rand said, "just as long as I'm sheriff here."

"Which may not be long at all," McAffee said. His walking stick rode around in an arc; he headed for the door. "You made a bad mistake, mollycoddlin' this black. You won't forget it. You can't even swallow it. Farris, when I'm done, you'll eat it."

Chapter 14

CLAY reached his ranch late in the afternoon, wearing a greatcoat over his natty suit. It was a tailored woolen suit with a dark vest buttoned over a ruffled shirt. A black cravat circled the high collar. Under the hat his hair was slicked down with oil.

He found Ben Harmony by the sound of the ax. Ben Harmony was trimming planks. String-pegged stakes marked the outlines of future cabin-room floors.

Ben Harmony's plaid sleeves were rolled up, revealing the red underwear beneath. Clay said, "Aren't you dressed yet?"

"Do I appear to be dressed?"

"Well," Clay said, "aren't you coming?"

Ben leaned on his axhandle and looked at him as if Clay were slightly crazy. "Coming where?"

"To the big party. At my house."

Ben Harmony grunted. "Chico, the only way I could get into a party at your house would be on a plate."

"All of you, or just your head?"

"What's that supposed to mean?"

"It means you're a fool. It means you're too damned sensitive. He let you go, didn't he? Just because Littlejack's dim in the head and McAffee's an old curmudgeon doesn't mean the whole country's down on you. You're making up lines where no lines are drawn."

"The lines are drawn," Ben Harmony said, "and I don't cross them. That's the way I stay alive, Chico."

"How do you know? Have you ever tried?"

Ben gave him a dismal look. Clay said, "What's the matter, Ben? Too good for us?"

"Don't taunt me, Chico. I'm in no mood for it. Let's just say I haven't got any formal clothes to wear."

"We'll scare up something."

"No," Ben Harmony said. "Listen, if it was anybody else but your old man, I might just come. But not this one."

"Why? What's between you and him?"

"Nothing that'd interest you. It happened a long, long time ago. Before you were even born."

"Before I was born, you weren't more than five."

"Old enough to learn the difference between Rand and Harmony, be that as it may."

Clay said, "I'm half a mind to get off this horse and pound a hole in your skull to find out what's inside."

"Don't, Chico. You've got enough trouble in your own life without going around digging up mine or anybody else's. Now get out of here—go on to your party. Somebody's got to look after these half-froze cows and build you a house to live in." He lifted his palm gravely. "Hail and farewell."

"Aagh," Clay said. He reined the horse around more savagely than he needed to and drummed away.

At six o'clock he drove the family buggy into Williams Street and presented himelf at Colonel McAffee's door.

Lavender swept the door open with a flourish. Clay said, "Howdy."

"Do you have an appointment?"

"No," he said.

"I'm afraid I never see anyone without an appointment."

"I see. Well, what would you say to six o'clock on Saturday night?"

"That would be fine," she said. "What time is it?"

"Six o'clock on Saturday night."

"Think of that." She beckoned with her fingers and stepped back.

"Where's the colonel?"

"Somewhere with that man with the funny eyes."

"Shoumacher?"

"I never remember his name," she said. It amused him, and she said, "That's a nice laugh."

He backed up against the door to push it shut, all the while holding her with a grave look. "Why do you have to look so beautiful?"

She went away from him, into the small drawing room, into which the colonel had crowded all the furniture of his own and his late son; the room was stuffed with settees and velvet chairs and knickknacks. Clay picked a path through it to the window, pulled a drapery aside and looked out. "That horse isn't used to hauling a buggy. I wouldn't want him to bolt for it—we'd better go soon."

"Are you frightened of that, really?"

He grinned, not looking at her. "It's just that the party's in our honor, and if I don't take you out of here pretty quick, we may not get there at all." He came back to her and slipped his arms around her little waist. He said, "Remember the first time I sparked you?"

"The box social."

"And I bid Bobby Rivers up to four dollars for your box lunch. Outbid him, too."

"An outrageous sum."

He kissed the tip of her nose. "I have got it bad," he said. "I put your face on every woman I see."

She said very seriously, "I do love you, Clay."

"Mm-hmm."

"But I'm worried about you."

"I seem to be the kind women worry about."

"My grandfather," she said. "He's been acting peculiarly."

"Never mind," he said. "He's like a dog that barks with one end and wags with the other. He—"

"That's what I mean, Clay. He's been too nice to me. He hasn't said a word against our engagement all week. He even told me he's going to the party tonight."

Clay had to think about that. He said, "Sometimes people scare me. They're so damned complicated."

Lavender gave him her arm. He took her outside and gave her a hand up; she got into the buggy and drew her coat around her shoulders. Clay settled on the seat beside her—he pulled her toward him, and she said, "Not here," smiling, looking prim in the shadows. "We're in a public place."

"Giddap."

Farris Rand had ordered the coming evening as a field general would plan a campaign. Señora Dominguez had arranged the house; her army of hired girls had dusted and swept, set out the crystal and damask. The full quarter of beef had spent the day slow-roasting in Señora Dominguez's kitchen, and at six the señora's two brawny sons had delivered it to Rand's back door. It stood in the kitchen, ready for carving. Decanters of wine lined the sideboard shelves, and the gentlemen's bar was arranged on the massive oak table in the parlor. Even the glass eyes of the twelve-point buck had been dusted and polished. Susan Rand's finest silver was on display. The china was laid out in rows for the buffet. Señora Dominguez had commandeered every respectable chair in the neighborhood for which there was space on the ground floor of the house. Magnums of 1883 White Seal champagne cooled in buckets of ice trimmed from the creeks.

Shortly after six o'clock Susan Rand came downstairs in a pale blue satin dress. Alone with her for a brief time in the parlor, the sheriff regarded her through the blue haze of his cigar smoke. He offered her a wrapped package and spoke gruffly. "Before the others arrive."

She examined it with mild surprise. "Shall I open it?"

"I'd be pleased if you would."

"Under the circumstances I don't know that I ought to accept a gift from you."

"It won't bite you." The sheriff's smile was dry. His moustache was waxed; he wore a burgundy dinner jacket with a shawl collar. Lamplight reflected small golden slivers in his eyes. "I had it shipped from New York."

It made her shoot a glance at him. "Then you thought of it quite some time ago."

"Yes."

"Perhaps you've changed your mind since you ordered it."

"Nothing's changed," he said. "Open it."

She undid the wrapping with care, and lifted out the contents—a mahogany music box. He found it hard to make out her expression. She lifted the lid, and a light-spirited tune tinkled from the mechanism, "The Londonderry Air." It made her smile involuntarily. Pasted into the lid was a four-color lithograph of a sylvan landscape, farmhouse and fence, a friendly visitor riding through the gate.

"Thank you, Farris. It's thoughtful."

"But no substitute for Clay's hand on the piano, is it?"

She' said, "Let's not talk about that now."

And the guests began to arrive. Some came afoot, but most of them pulled up in rigs and buggies. Emmett Smyley and his wife arrived in the doctor's enclosed hansom, a weather-resistant vehicle that could be driven from the inside with the reins threaded through a slot; it had been one of Smyley's earliest investments, prompted by the numerous emergency calls that took him out in all kinds of weather.

One couple, the Dinwiddies, came in an open victoria. Dinwiddie could usually be expected to do the unexpected.

A liveried Mexican took their rigs and led them away to hitch them along the street. The guests came up to the door smiling tentatively. Beards and sideburns and painstakingly coiffured hairdresses, silk opera hats and the greatest finery of attire that could be mustered in the town of Ocotillo assembled here. (There were occasional incongruities. Mrs. Dinwiddie wore a postilion hat. Mrs. Littlejack, a stout woman, arrived in a Gainsborough sort of gown that swept the floor.)

There were greetings and "Lay off your things in the pantry, folks." Powdered and discreetly rouged, corseted in whalebone and carrying fans in their gloved hands, the ladies made a bright swirl of bustled and bustling color. Clay found himself separated from Lavender by the traffic. He stood near the sideboard and caught glimpses of her. She was somewhere in the shuffle, with her red hair tossing; he kept losing track of her. A bombardment of good wishes fell upon him, which he accepted as best he could until Clyde Little-jack loomed up and said, "I want to offer you congratulations and good luck, kid. You ain't going to need the congratulations, but I got a feeling you might use the luck."

"Thank you," Clay said coolly. He was less than pleased by Littlejack's presence here, but evidently this night was to be a brief time of truce; his father had made temporary peace with his enemies. There seemed to be an unspoken agreement that politics would not be discussed. For a while no one broke it. Nevertheless, the hearty gusto and good cheer were uncomfortably false, and Clay quickly fortified himself with what Harry Greiff told him was half a pint of puma sweat. While he drank, in the midst of loud, forced gaiety, he had an image of Ben Harmony, out there on the ranch, probably cooking his meager supper over an open fire and draping a horse-sweaty saddle blanket around him for warmth in the open lean-to. The sheriff had given Ben Harmony a tongue-lashing after the shooting incident in the Occidental, and since that night Ben Harmony had not come into town at all. It was October sixteenth, and the night winds across the hills were coming bitter cold: this morning Clay had chopped a thin rime of ice from the creek to water his stock. Thinking about that, he only half heard the congratulations that battered him back into the corner by the sideboard. Bobby Rivers came up, gangly and towheaded, with a drink in his hand, and regarded Clay with undisguised envy. Bobby looked awkward in his stiff collar; his smile was sickly. Clay shook off his reverie and greeted Bobby Rivers warmly, savoring a sense of revenge in the generosity with which he forgave Bobby his trespasses.

Dr. Smyley remarked to Littlejack, "Two fellows your size would make a crowd, Clyde." Mayor Foster, who was very fat, was discoursing on the subject of William Jennings Bryan, the boy orator of the Platte, who by now was at the end of his vigorous campaign; on the third of November the national election would pit him against McKinley. Foster puffed out his enormous belly and said, "Free silver again? We'll just have to tighten our belts, that's all." It went on that way—desultory talk and pleasantries. Udray, who had driven in from Rafter Cross, reached the bar with Clay's father and said, "I don't come to these things often, Farris. Can't take too much of saying nice things I don't mean to people who don't believe me. But I'll say this to you, Clay, and mean it. You're a man to be proud of. I'd be honored to ride the river with you. I wish you all the best things, you and your girl."

"Thanks, Mr. Udray."

Udray turned back to the sheriff. "Somebody ran off six head of my stock last night."

"Did you recognize any of them?"

Udray shrugged. "Cows all look the same to me."

Clay's father laughed politely at the cattleman's little joke; the two gray men drifted away with their drinks.

Clay glimpsed Lavender's red hair passing the door. The ladies seemed to have gathered in the dining room. Men circulated around Clay's position; Dr. Smyley came by, putting on his glasses, hooking them over one ear at a time. "Hell of a big night for you, Clay."

"Yes, sir, it is."

Harry Greiff moved in, looking out of place in his dress suit. The doctor said to him, "Those clothes on you look about like horns on a filly. Hell of a fraud you are."

Greiff laughed. He was off duty tonight, already a little drunk. Clay watched him pour a stiff drink. The deputy's thick brows overhung his eyes, so bushy that his expressions were invisible. "Don't ever become a lawman, son," he advised, and lurched away.

Dr. Smyley looked across the foyer toward the dining room, where guests filed in and out. "How about a bite to eat, son? All this standing around and jawing makes me hungry as all hell."

There was a jumble of finding places to sit and eat. Lavender smiled at Clay, but a woman took the seat beside her; Clay elevated his arms and shook his head with a grin and took his supper back into the parlor. A rancher joined him and entertained him with talk of hanging Billy Cordell. Clay tried hard to put some show of interest on his face. Finally he said, "I don't think there'll be any hanging, Mr. Mossgrove. Billy didn't kill anybody. Excuse me?"

He got up and ate alone by the sideboard. He put his plate away, caught Señora Dominguez's warm wink, and backed surreptitiously into the kitchen. Feeling drunk, he went outside into the cold open air.

He threw his head back and breathed deep. He could hear the clatter of dishes; someone laughed. The chilly dark bit into him so that his flesh rippled, but he stood there with his hands in his pockets, frowning. *It's supposed to be our night,* he was thinking, but the specters of Ben Harmony and the election confused it all. Not that Ben Harmony had done anything that Clay would not have done in his shoes, or so Clay thought, but Ben had driven a wedge into the town. He was on everybody's mind, even if no one spoke his name.

After a while the cold got to him. He went back inside, passed Señora Dominguez's broad rump, and palmed the knob of the dining room door to pull it open. But it already stood a few inches ajar, and he did not open it farther just then, for a woman was talking beyond the door, confiding in a low voice to someone with her.

"Look at him, handsome as you please. He's standing over there thinking of the time when he didn't seduce Cavendish's wife. Heaven only knows what would have come of that poor woman if they hadn't decided to move to San Francisco. And it's easy to see it won't be long before young Clay turns into the spitting image of him."

The woman's voice was horsey. It wasn't hard to identify Mrs. Dinwiddie by the bluntness of her tongue. She went on. "Farris was always hard to swallow, but he's turning into a real liability."

The second woman said, "It's a wonder Susan puts up with it."

"There's no knowing those two. It's not a family—it's a tactical alliance."

Clay pressed his lips together. He swung the door open and tramped into the dining room, never glancing at Mrs. Dinwiddie by the door. He walked right past, across the room and into the parlor.

Harry Greiff grasped his arm at the door. "Here you are. Where you been hiding? Come on, everybody's waiting for you."

In his father's parlor the champagne had been opened and poured. Clay's father stood by the table with one arm across Lavender's shoulders; when Clay came forward, the sheriff lifted his glass.

"Ladies and gentlemen. To these two fine young people. To Lavender—" he bowed toward her—"and to my son."

The guests gestured and drank and came crowding around, pounding Clay's back, congratulating them both. He felt half smothered. Lavender squeezed in beside him, and he held her around the waist, seeing her smile but unable to hear what she said. Past the top of her head he saw his father, beaming, drinking champagne. Clay listened vaguely to the people pay lip service, but his attention was on his father's face. He couldn't shake loose Mrs. Dinwiddie's talk.

Colonel McAffee arrived. It was easy to tell, because the volume of talk diminished like a quick intake of breath. The crowd parted to let him through. McAffee was all dressed up in wing collar and cravat. His nose looked like a vein-and-artery chart in a textbook. He lurched slightly. "Not too late to toast the bride and groom to be, am I?"

Someone pressed a drink into the colonel's hand. He lifted

his face. "Libation now and then's supposed to be good for the health. Prevents—what do you call it?—cirrhosis. Mighty fine champagne, Farris. My, my, I'm delighted to see all these wonderful people gathered together in peace. Farris, treasure it. It may blow all to bits tomorrow. But we'll observe our uneasy truce for the nonce, hmm? Here's to you, my lovely granddaughter, and here's to my prospective grandson-in-law. Youth is a priceless thing, and it's my profound hope you'll never regret exchanging it for premature matrimonial middle-age, be that as it may."

The colonel drank his toast and lifted his glass once more. "And here's to your father, young man. May he have the grace to retire with honor from the field come the third of next month."

McAffee almost choked, laughing, on a mouthful of champagne.

Dinwiddie adjusted his pince-nez and remarked softly, dryly, "Colonel, you'd give a speech anywhere you could gather an audience." There was a jittery run of laughter. Through a hole in the crowd, Clay fixed his eyes on his father's feet. The sheriff had forsaken his polished boots tonight; he wore a pair of black pumps that Clay had never seen before. Beneath the fabric of her dress he could feel the soft warmth of Lavender's skin. She was looking up into his face. Her eyes shone. Harry Greiff, getting progressively drunker, yelled out boisterously: "Hot beef and cold booze. What more do we need?" The men were perspiring. McAffee was absorbed by a knot of people.

Dinwiddie launched into an impersonation of William Jennings Bryan, with gestures, impudently accurate. "You shall not press down upon the brow of labor this crown of thorns, you shall not crucify mankind upon a cross of gold!" Nobody laughed much—Bryan was the Westerners' candidate—but the town had learned to tolerate Dinwiddie's waywardness and no one took offense.

Clay guided Lavender toward the door; she submitted with an agreeable smile. Clay's mother met them in the doorway. Lavender said, "We thought we'd go out and see the moonlight. Will you join us?"

Mrs. Rand cocked her head toward them. "I think I've seen all my moonlight. You two go ahead."

They went out on the front porch. As soon as Clay closed the door, Lavender said, "What's wrong?"

"What do you mean?"

"You look like the last rose of summer."

"It's nothing." He turned her in the circle of his arms. "Just looking at you brings me all the way back from wherever I was."

"I'm glad. It didn't look like a nice place."

He adored her. He whispered, "Only one way to say I love you—and that's not enough." He kissed her gently. She looked lidded and dreamy. He said, "You are all I want."

She snuggled against him and spoke with the side of her face against his chest. "I always believed in love at first sight, but it took three years for us to decide. Do you remember when I almost left here? When Mama died, I didn't think the house could hold the grief. I hated my grandfather then—I had to get away."

"I came with you," he said. "To the vestibule on the train—to say goodbye. We never got it said, did we? I couldn't see me walking nobly out of your life. I had to make you stay."

"I'm glad you did," she said. "But sometimes I'm afraid of your power over me, Clay. I guess I'm selfish. I just don't want to be hurt."

A buggy came rutting down the street. It broke them apart, but Clay held on to her hand. The buggy drew up at the gate, and Philip Shoumacher dismounted, holding up both hands to help a woman down.

"He's certainly late," said Lavender. "Is that his wife, I wonder?"

"I don't know. I've never met her."

"She looks like a shrew."

The woman was small and bowed. "Don't be unkind," Clay murmured. Shoumacher and his wife ascended the porch steps. The editor tilted up one side of his mouth.

"I hope we didn't interrupt."

"Come inside," Clay said with no great show of friendliness. "Mrs. Shoumacher? I'm Clay Rand."

"Yes. I'm happy to meet you." She was a strict little woman with a chapped mouth.

"Miss McAffee, Mrs. Shoumacher."

Shoumacher said, "You got the introduction in the wrong order, you know," and followed his wife inside.

Lavender whispered in Clay's ear, "What a sour pair."

"Maybe he's got something to be sour about."

"You mean his wife?" She giggled.

Clay shrugged. He had never been able to decide what he thought of Shoumacher.

Inside, the gathering pulsed with loud talk. The sheriff stood by the gun case and held himself rigidly aloof from the ribaldry. The men had become loose and loud, intruding upon the shell of Farris Rand's indifference. Dinwiddie had pushed the Occidental's professor off the piano stool and was playing "Garry Owen" very fast, with a certain flair. Whether or not it was meant to have any particular significance was known only to Dinwiddie, who had a strange sense of justice: "Garry Owen" had been Custer's regimental theme.

The sheriff tried to make his voice sound courteous when he said, "Good evening," to Philip Shoumacher.

"Pour syrup on waffles, Sheriff, not on me."

The sheriff put on a little smile, in acknowledgment of the declared truce, but he said, "Your welcome here is fragile at best. Take it easy."

Shoumacher's hand fluttered in a conciliatory way. He changed the subject. "My wife, Ethel."

Farris Rand dipped his head. "Ma'am."

She said, "My husband promised he would try not to disgrace me this evening." She gave Shoumacher a thin-lipped smile. He stared at her, but she turned blithely and began to chat with Dinwiddie at the piano.

The sheriff deliberately turned away from Shoumacher, but Shoumacher was not inclined to release him. "If our presence isn't desired, you'll have to say it out loud."

The sheriff said, "You invited yourself to come. You may invite yourself to leave whenever it pleases you."

Swollen at all times, Shoumacher's eyes had a gloss on them. He was never far out of reach of a whiskey bottle; he was, as usual, a little high. "I took it as a simple oversight that you neglected to invite us."

"Take it as you like."

Shoumacher waved, encompassing McAffee and Littlejack and all the others. "Why wasn't I included in your temporary armistice?"

"Let's just put it this way—it's always seemed prudent to me to drink upstream from your kind."

Shoumacher's wife cut in. "Should I resent that insult for you, dear?"

The sheriff turned away slowly. Someone laughed dispiritedly. Near Clay, Harry Greiff said low in his throat, "See that? I thought Shoumacher was going to cry."

Susan Rand went to the front door for a breath of air. Udray and Colonel McAffee were talking silver politics in the foyer; they gave her a guilty look, and she said, "Gentlemen, please go ahead and smoke your cigars."

Someone came to the parlor door and called Udray's name. The rancher touched McAffee's arm and went away. Left alone with McAffee, Susan Rand said, "I've been hoping to have a chance to talk with you."

"Of course." McAffee was a curious man, crisp yet roundabout, besotted yet clever. "Fine lad, your son."

"Thank you."

"That doesn't just happen."

"Thank you again."

"You're as troubled as I am. About this—wedding."

"Perhaps we shouldn't pry," said Susan Rand.

"Our responsibility. Well, she's a grown woman, eighteen, old enough for marriage by the custom of this country. But I've never pushed her into anything—and least of all this." He moved a step closer and pitched his voice lower.

"Shock to her, her father dying young, and then her mother two years ago. Took her a while to get her bearings. She's an honest girl, a good girl. Any man who puts his faith in her will have it rewarded. But she's picked a bad time for this—we all know that."

"I agree with you, Colonel, but there doesn't seem to be much for us to do about it now but accept it."

"I tried not to encourage her seeing your boy. Not because he's bad, you understand. But Lavender's still batting around searching for things. Mother's death uprooted her, don't you know. I felt, still do feel, until she's made up her mind about a good many things, she shouldn't tie herself down."

"Naturally."

"Quite right, Mrs. Rand." His jaw tended to chop up and

down when he talked. He looked past her shoulder. When she looked, she found Clay and Lavender coming forward.

Colonel McAffee wheezed, snorted, rearranged his catarrh, and finally said, "Like to have a talk with you two. Seems a good time for it."

Susan Rand said quickly, "It's likely to be a fruitless discussion, Colonel. Perhaps we'd better not."

Clay said, "What kind of talk?"

The colonel chuckled. "Suspicious. Maybe that's not a bad thing. How old are you?"

"Going on twenty."

"Nineteen. My granddaughter's eighteen."

Lavender said, "I know what you're going to say, but it won't change anything."

"Possibly. But it's got to be said. You are eighteen years of age and—"

"My mother," Clay said, "was eighteen when my parents were married. Isn't that right, Mother?"

His mother said, "That's hardly the—"

McAffee said, "And how old was your father? But no matter." He wiped his mouth. "Forgive me. I'm a little drunker than usual tonight. Listen here, son, I've got no grudge against you, except maybe that darky you've cursed us with. Just between these four walls it's one particular curse that may work in my favor—you do get my meaning?—but man to man, Clay, you've picked a bad, bad time for all this. It can embarrass your father, embarrass me as well. Might be wise if you'd look into your conscience and tell me if you've really thought it out."

"Before you appeal to my conscience," said Clay, "maybe you'd better examine your own."

Lavender said, "Be still, both of you. Grandfather, you promised me."

"So I did," McAffee muttered, puffing out his cheeks.

Susan Rand said, "My husband is coming."

The sheriff arrived, found the four of them arrayed in the foyer, and said without preamble, "Colonel, I'd appreciate it if you'd not make any more speeches tonight."

McAffee reared back. "I resent arbitrary attempts to muzzle me."

The sheriff shook his head sadly. "Can it be that our pool of able men is so impoverished that they couldn't find anyone better than you to run against me?" Without waiting for an answer, he went through the front door and out.

"Why—" McAffee thundered. Lavender took him by the elbow and steered him back inside. Clay chuckled and went with them.

Left alone in the foyer, Susan pressed both palms to her temples. After a moment she went outside after her husband, showing her anger. He stood in the shadows at the end of the veranda, touching the points of his moustache. She approached him; he reached for her arm, but she disengaged it. "Was that necessary, Farris?"

"Maybe not. I'm sick of him." His dry, stained fingers smelled of cigars. He dropped his hand. "I don't know why you and I have to go on hurting each other."

"Don't you?"

"Susan, I don't think I'll be able to stay in this house if you're not in it."

It made her face him. His jaw was set; he said, "You're very beautiful tonight."

"You don't often look for the right thing to say."

"Sometimes a man's got to be careful. When you're in the woods getting close to a wild animal, you don't want to talk suddenly or move fast. If you startle it, it may bolt away."

"Now I'm a wild animal, am I?"

"You know what I meant."

Her face was soft in the dim light. "I don't think I've ever understood you."

"I think you understand me very well."

"You're part preacher and part gypsy. I can never anticipate your moods."

He said, "There ought to be some advantage in that."

"At my age excitement isn't worth much " she said.

"Don't make yourself older than you are."

"It's important to a woman to know where she stands. I wanted to stand by you. But you refused me a place to stand. I can't be secure in my trust, Farris—I can't trust you any more at all."

He said, "We haven't got the happiness we wanted, but I don't believe we can go back and start again. All we can do is pick up the pieces that are left and make what we can out of them. Maybe that can be enough."

"Enough for what?"

"Susan, if you took one step toward me, I'd walk a hundred miles to meet you."

It was a moment that needed something other than a quick answer. It asked for the kind of decision that would have to be honored for a lifetime.

Someone inside the house was playing the piano. She listened intently for a few seconds; it was not Clay's hand. The cold wind swept across the porch, roughing up the bare branches above the veranda roof. Shadows moved across the lamplit curtains. The party was noisy and busy.

Susan said, "It's the wrong time for this. Don't take advantage of my confusion. There's too much going on all at once, and I've lost my balance."

"But we'll talk about it soon."

"All right, Farris."

He watched her walk back into the house. She moved with grace and pride, bowing her head and smiling to greet someone in the foyer.

Farris Rand finished his cigar, listening to the wind rush through the dark town. Light shone along the silver mane of his hair. His patrician face was composed; he seemed at ease.

He turned into the house, found his drink, and returned to the gathering of men in the parlor.

Dinwiddie was banging out a saloon rag. The sheriff stopped in the doorway; he watched his son make a path through the crowd, carefully balancing a brim-full glass of champagne. Clay's face was flushed; he was tipsy and loose. He spoke to Dinwiddie, who nodded and wiped his brow with his sleeve and made way at the piano bench. Clay sat down and flexed his fingers.

Farris Rand put his shoulder against the wall and watched from twenty feet away. He felt weight beside him and glanced that way. His wife had stopped in the doorway; she was watching Clay with such close attention that she seemed to have stopped breathing.

Clay brooded on the keyboard while he drank half an inch of champagne, and then abruptly he made a brief, angry remark and stood up without having touched the piano.

Susan cast her eyes down. The sheriff's expression underwent a small change. She glanced at him and moved away; he advanced into the crowd, toward a knot of men standing at the bar, attentive to Philip Shoumacher, who was investing his talk with pious unction. Words flowed out of him viscously, like thick, oozing axle grease. The sheriff caught one passage:

"Violence answers no questions. It's the easiest thing in the world to get into a fight—it takes a better man by far to know when not to fight. Don't you see, we've got to—"

The sheriff didn't catch the rest of it, but he moved toward the bar with choppy strides and cut in. "I didn't offer this house as a forum for your asinine opinions, Mr. Shoumacher."

"Indeed? I say what I think, Sheriff."

"An overrated virtue," Farris Rand commented. Two men stepped back, leaving an opening. The sheriff spoke across it.

"You're dull when you get drunk. I don't think anyone's entertained. Yield the floor, will you?" The sheriff grimaced, turned around, and began to walk away.

"Don't turn your back on me!" cried Shoumacher.

The sheriff turned back. "No?" he asked. "Well, then, I suppose you're right. A man shouldn't turn his back on you."

Shoumacher's face brightened to crimson. His rigid smile cracked. His bravado mounted. "When a man becomes too powerful, he forgets the basic courtesies. You're a crude case in point."

The sheriff refused to be baited, and Shoumacher said, "We've had enough of you, do you hear me? We want your resignation." It was an intolerant whine.

"Who," the sheriff snapped, "is 'we'? Identify yourselves."

His eyes prowled from face to face. "No? Gentlemen, we weren't going to talk politics tonight, and so all I'll say is this. On every ship one man has to be on the bridge, and I happen to be that man here. If it doesn't suit you, you'll have your opportunity to express yourself on Election Day."

He thrust a cigar in his mouth. "You're smug, Shoumacher, and you're stupid. I didn't make the laws here. If you don't like them, change them—but don't fling your tantrums at me. You've made it clear how you feel about this town—and I can only observe that if it's as rotten as you claim it is, then it's the good citizens like you who've rotted it up."

Harry Greiff said thickly, "Hear, hear."

Showing his disgust, the sheriff said, "Shoumacher, look in the mirror sometime."

"What'll I see, Sheriff?"

"Excrement." The sheriff's reply was businesslike.

Shoumacher's answer to it was voluminous. His voice trembled, roared, and toppled. At the end of it he howled, "Murderers are the most conceited people on earth, Rand, and you are chief among them. You're a bloodthirsty pig!"

When Shoumacher ran out of things to say, Farris Rand removed the cigar from his tight-lipped mouth and grunted. He said, "Your assumption of infallibility only proves that your mind is closed."

Clyde Littlejack reached the near edge of the group, head cocked over on one side. "What? Huh?"

The sheriff glanced at him. "I'll translate. Only fools are dead-sure, Clyde. Does that answer you?"

"I agree with what Shoumacher said there," Littlejack said.

"The hell you do. You didn't understand half of it."

Dinwiddie said mildly, "Even Clyde has the right to an opinion, Farris."

"Even Clyde," the sheriff agreed. "Now I will tell you all this. When you get a tough steak, you need a sharp knife. If you people think Stanton McAffee can cut anything harder than butter, then you'll deserve what happens to you."

McAffee had been sitting half-asleep in the corner. He bounced to his feet. "Hold on—hold on. Ladies and gentlemen, honored citizens—"

Harry Greiff, beside him, pushed him down into his chair. The colonel's eyes rolled up, and he subsided, mumbling.

The sheriff said, "Shoumacher, say good night."

Dinwiddie said, "Here's your head, Phil, don't hurry out." He laughed softly.

The sheriff added, "Set foot in my house again and I'll set the dogs on you."

Dinwiddie, still laughing, said, "I didn't know you had any dogs, Farris."

"I'll buy a pack of them if I have to."

Harry Greiff stumbled forward and grasped Shoumacher by the shoulder. "Goodbye, friend." With a stiffened forefinger against Shoumacher's chest, he pushed the man backward through the door.

Somehow Mrs. Shoumacher appeared, carrying topcoats. She looked as though she had no lips. She draped the editor's coat over his shoulders without speaking, clapped the hat on his head, and steered him away. His rising protests rolled back through the hall.

It broke the party apart. The Dinwiddies gathered Colonel McAffee and took him home. Simmering anger brooded in the colonel's flaccid, half-conscious face. The guests left by ones and twos, Clay escorting Lavender to the buggy, Little-jack muttering to himself as he left, Harry Greiff holding his head painfully. "Sleep well," Harry Greiff said.

Farris Rand replied, "I always do."

Chapter 15

BEN Harmony had declined to come into town with him, so Clay had to load the wagon himself. After he lashed down the heavy load of planks, he laid his hat on the wagon seat and let the cold wind rough up his hair. Sweat logged his shirt, and the chill made him drag down his coat and shoulder into it. A few cottonball clouds scudded across the horizon, but the blazing sky made the October cold all the more brutal.

He turned up the fleece collar and fastened the coat buckles, climbed onto the high seat and tooled the laden wagon out of the lumberyard. The yardmaster gave him a lazy hand salute and disappeared inside his shack with a pencil in his teeth. Clay guided the wagon along the ruts of the alley and made his turn into Partridge Street, ducking his head against the brittle sting of the wind.

A loose sheet of newspaper flapped along the street. The team shied; Clay spoke roughly and looked over his shoulder to see if the load had shifted. It had not. He took the whip from its socket and cracked it in the air. The team plodded forward, paying the lash no mind, and Clay put it away; he settled down on the seat with his shoulders hunched up and his hat pulled down, work gloves on his fists and dust in his eyes.

Philip Shoumacher stood outside the door of the *Enterprise,* watching. When Clay came within hailing distance, Shoumacher lifted his arm. "Have you got a minute?"

"What for?"

"Come inside."

"I've got to get this lumber out to the ranch."

"It's important," Shoumacher said. His frog eyes were veined and weary. "I won't keep you long."

Not sure what to make of it, Clay turned in and hitched the team. When he climbed onto the walk, Shoumacher turned his back and minced inside. Clay scratched his jaw and heard the glove rasp against stubble: at nineteen he was already inheriting his father's abrasive beard.

Behind the counter the press stood open, ready for inking; reams of newsprint waited in bales, and a page proof lay uncreased on the platen, predominant with advertisements, as was the custom for front pages.

"Good morning." That was Dinwiddie's caustic voice; until now Clay had not noticed him. Dinwiddie stood by the front window, stovepipe hat square across his brows.

Clay glanced quickly at Shoumacher. There was something here that the two of them knew and he did not. He stopped where he was, cautious and uncertain. Shoumacher gave him a bloodshot look and tried to beam amiably; Dinwiddie kept a covert scrutiny against him. Dinwiddie smothered a yawn.

Shoumacher said, "I've been wanting to talk to you about what happened at your father's house the other night."

"That was between you and him."

"Things aren't that simple anymore," Shoumacher said. "I think perhaps I can help you."

"I don't need any help," Clay said.

"I think you do."

"Why?"

At that point Dinwiddie walked over to the editor's desk, sat down, and crossed his legs with a sour expression on his face and a faraway stare that indicated his desire to dissociate himself from whatever was to transpire.

Shoumacher spoke in a confidential way. "There are a few things you ought to know, Clay."

Dinwiddie squirmed on the swivel chair. "Maybe we ought to—"

"Never mind," Shoumacher said, aside. He said to Clay, "There are people who go all through life convinced that things only belong to the man who can get a strong grip on them. You don't get what you deserve, they say. You only get what you can grab. They're clever, these people. They find excuses for that kind of behavior by slinging around all sorts of moralistic arguments about honor and pride and self-sufficiency and individualism—but when you get right down to it, it's all a smoke screen. It's part of our history that we tend to act first and dream up high-sounding justifications afterward."

Clay pushed his hat back. "In the first place, I don't like being talked down to. I'm not a kid. And in the second place, you've strung a lot of words together, but you haven't said anything, and I've got a load of lumber to take home."

"I'm coming to it, Clay. A good advocate has to lay the groundwork first."

Dinwiddie kept crossing and uncrossing his legs. He didn't look at anyone.

Shoumacher said, "Your old man has the wool pulled over your eyes."

"What?"

Shoumacher settled back and almost purred. "It's better to find these things out early. After all, you have a right to make your own choices, but a man can't do that unless he has all the information bearing on the case. I'm only acting in your own interests—I've taken a liking to you, and I want to see you be your own man."

Clay made a face. "Am I supposed to believe you?"

"Believe what you wish. I only want to be your friend."

"You'd make a curious kind of left-handed friend."

Dinwiddie ransacked the desk drawers until he found a bottle of whiskey. He gestured with it. "Whiskey helps keep the bowels open. In this country that's important." He helped himself.

Shoumacher said, "First, then, I don't suppose this will come as news to you, but your father has a reputation as a ladies' man. Now—"

"It doesn't," Clay snapped.

"Doesn't what?"

"Come as news to me." Clay made his face look sleepy and tough, but he was remembering Dinwiddie's wife and the gossip he'd overheard. His glance roamed toward Dinwiddie and shifted back to Shoumacher—he saw the disappointment on Shoumacher's face.

Shoumacher cleared his throat. Dinwiddie, smiling as if he felt sick, turned his palms up. Clay said to Shoumacher, "You're a malicious old woman," and turned away.

"Wait."

"What for?"

Shoumacher said, "I regret these circumstances very deeply, Clay, but I can't just keep silent. Tolerance is not always a virtue. Tolerance of evil is itself an evil. I'd think this might open your eyes. Your father is no ivory god. Every man has his weaknesses, and God knows Farris Rand's no exception. The longer you idolize him, the worse it will be for you."

Clay couldn't help uttering a brief bark of snorting laughter.

Shoumacher was oblivious. "I've watched you, Clay, and it's all too apparent to me that you lap up everything your father puts in front of you. Before long you'll be as petrified as those trees on the desert east of here. Your values will be as fossil as your father's. The law can do no wrong, even when it commits roughshod murders—Clay, somebody had to talk to you. I'm sorry if you hate me for it, but I don't want to see you start a new generation of men who'd rather use a gun than use their heads. They're out of kilter, Clay. They're relics. If you start thinking the way they think, you're lost."

Dinwiddie upended the bottle and sucked from it. His eyes were closed. Shoumacher rubbed his hands primly. "Your father's character leaves everything to be desired. He's lied to you all these years, by making you believe he was an honorable man."

Clay said, "You've got more nerve than I reckoned, gambling that I wouldn't tear you apart for talking like that."

"I give you more credit than that. What would it solve?" Shoumacher's face colored under Clay's stare.

Dinwiddie crossed his legs and began to laugh off-key; he said, "It's not without its element of humor, is it?"

Shoumacher was stiff and bookish. "I see nothing funny in it. This boy's life may depend on the decisions he makes right now."

Dinwiddie's unhappy face stirred. "Don't take him too seriously, Clay. Don't take anything too seriously. Hell, what if your old man does have a case of galloping satyriasis? You can't throw out the baby with the bathwater. Maybe your father's no worse and no better than a lot of us."

Shoumacher said, "By what curious process did you arrive at that conclusion?"

"It's not a conclusion. It's a surmise. But your evidence is no better than mine."

Shoumacher put on his dead-fish smile. "Isn't it?"

Clay said, "I'm going."

"Not just yet." It was Shoumacher's tone of voice that arrested Clay. Shoumacher got tough. "Did you ever wonder why your father has gone out of his way to make things easy for your Negro friend?"

"Say what you mean, Phil," Dinwiddie said, "or shut up."

"I will. Clay, you don't want to hear this, and I don't want to say it, but things have gone too far. I'm printing the facts in tonight's newspaper, and I only thought it would be fair to advise you in advance."

"In advance of what?" Clay said. "What facts? Jesus, you can drive a fellow crazy with your roundabout rigamarole."

Shoumacher turned around and reached across the counter. He dragged the printed page proof from the platen, reversed it, and laid it on the counter backside up. The ink, still wet, glistened. "See for yourself."

Dinwiddie got up from his chair and came across the room to peer over Clay's shoulder. Clay read slowly. Dinwiddie murmured, "I bow to your unfortunate, abysmal honesty, Phil. I never thought you could be this low. Where in hell did you unearth this piece of dirt?"

"I did some prospecting, by telegraph. I hit pay dirt in St. Louis."

A knotted muscle rippled in Clay's jaw. He lifted his face and stared at Shoumacher. His eyes looked like two holes burned in a blanket. He did not speak at first.

Shoumacher said, "Ben Harmony's mother was a Negro tramp in St. Louis. Rand kept her hidden away on a back street. Clay, I regret being the instrument in this. I particularly regret knowing that I've earned your hatred from this moment on. But it is the only way I know to save this community. The town must know the facts before it goes to the polls to elect the High Sheriff. It must know that Ben Harmony is your father's bastard son. Your half brother."

"Shut up," Clay breathed. "Just shut up."

Dinwiddie said, "This is life, Clay. About time we both got used to it."

"Keep your mouth off me."

Shoumacher stayed put, watching Clay, holding his breath.

His eyes seemed ready to pop out of his head. He said, "You must feel as if you'd been kicked by a mule. I'm sorry. I wish I knew how to be kind."

Clay's brows knitted. He looked at his fists as if they were unfamiliar objects. He didn't say anything; he turned right around and headed for the door, forgetting his hat. He pushed the door out of his way and went outside. His boot heels thrust back leaden echoes.

Dinwiddie pulled suicidally at the mouth of the bottle. When he put it down, he sagged into the chair, loose and beaten. "Why'd you have to do it, Phil?"

"It's the truth."

"I know, but—"

"There are no 'buts.' "

"You're throwing raw meat on the floor," Dinwiddie said. "When that paper hits Farris Rand's desk, you'll be looking for your head in a basket."

"I doubt it," Shoumacher said.

"Farris was right. You *are* smug."

"Am I?" Shoumacher said. He acted unconcerned.

"You could at least have gone to Farris privately and told him what you knew. You could have offered him a chance to withdraw from the election. You didn't have to go ahead and print it."

"That would be blackmail. Besides, why should I bargain when I've got a corner on the market?"

"You've made a mistake," Dinwiddie said. He stood up. "It may finish you in this town. Did you think of that?"

"Finish me?" Shoumacher shook his head. "I guess not. They'll be too busy crucifying Rand. As they must."

"I think it'll finish you," Dinwiddie insisted, heading for the door. "And being the rat I am, I'm deserting the sinking ship right now. Goodbye, Phil."

Dinwiddie adjusted his hat, went outside, took one last look through the doorway at Shoumacher, and hurried away.

Chapter 16

BEN Harmony was scratching a dose of poison oak he had picked up near camp. He insisted, "Are you sure?"

"Who was there? You or me? I heard what he said. I read the newspaper."

Ben said, "You know what I like about Shoumacher?"

"What?"

"Nothing."

"Shoumacher's a buzzard," Clay said.

"Sure. But don't forget that a buzzard can spot a helpless field mouse from five thousand feet up. Christ, I never meant to get the old man into anything like this."

"Then it's true," Clay muttered.

"Sure it is."

"You're my half brother."

Ben Harmony's mouth twisted. "I didn't think you'd like it much."

"You didn't think at all," Clay shouted. "Why the hell did you come here? You must have known it would come out."

"Simmer down."

"What?"

"Just ease off me, Chico. You can't make me feel any worse. Look, maybe I was just sick and tired of spending my life breaking horses for six bits a head. I never saw it chiseled on stone tablets that a man had to stay a thousand miles away from the only family he's got."

"But, for God's sake, why? What did you come for, Ben? What did you want?"

Ben Harmony's burly shoulders lifted and fell. A man who

thought best on his feet, he stalked to the loaded wagon and began to pitch lumber down, board by board. Clay stood back from the dust thrown up by the plunging planks. He dragged the backhand side of a glove across his face. The wind, bitter cold, sluiced down the hillsides. By the chopped-open creek his thirty-six cattle huddled.

Ben said, "You're pretty rocky. Grab some coffee off the fire there. Might settle you down. And don't complain about the coffee—someday you'll be old and weak yourself."

"Is that all you've got to say?" Clay demanded.

"What do you want me to say?" Ben got down off the wagon and began dragging loose boards off. The lumber pile on the ground was a disordered mess, uncharacteristic of Ben Harmony. He said, "Look, I'm Farris Rand's son, just like you are. What else do you want me to say?"

Clay shook his head mutely. Anger turned him away. He crouched by the fire and reached for the soot-black coffeepot. Today he realized dismally how little he knew about Ben Harmony—how little he knew about anybody. He had to think about it. Maybe Ben was only an uprooted soul to whom the only important thing was to find his place in the scheme of things—but if that was so, why had he kept silent so long? Beneath Ben's surface of impudent amusement was some obstinate resolve—to do what? Clay said as much: "You've got to tell me what you came here for. You owe it to me."

"I don't owe anybody anything," said Ben Harmony. "It's the other way around. But I'll tell you this much. I didn't come to blackmail the old man, and I didn't come to make trouble."

"Did you want him to admit out loud that he's your father?"

"Maybe. But it wouldn't be any good if I had to force him to admit it. And that's what Shoumacher's doing. If he publishes that story, it'll wipe all of us out—you can see that."

"But we can't stop him."

"Maybe," Ben Harmony said. He walked toward his horse, talking over his shoulder. "Who else knows about it? Who was there? Just you and Shoumacher?"

"Dinwiddie."

"Find him. Keep him from spreading it around."

"How?"

"Just do it, Chico. Ask me how later." Ben Harmony yanked the cinch tight, gathered the reins, and mounted.

"Where are you going?"

"To stop Shoumacher from printing it."

"There'll be hell to pay, Ben."

"Then I'll pay it. You get going, Chico." Ben Harmony settled his feet in the stirrups and lashed the horse. Clay's heart pounded. He watched Ben thunder away. In the front of his mind was the one certain piece of knowledge he had about Ben Harmony. Ben might ask Shoumacher to kill the story, and then again Ben might *tell* him, but one thing Ben would not do was beg him. Ben never begged.

Ben Harmony made a right turn and a left turn, passed the Occidental at a canter, and rode under the limb of a brown-leafed cottonwood. The chill wind stirred little puffs of dust in the street. In the open mouth of his blacksmith shop Clyde Littlejack stared unblinkingly at Ben Harmony. Ben went by without a glance and drew rein in front of the newspaper office. Down the street the big banner was fading in the window of the Canaanite Mission: "R E P E N T ." The adobe buildings along the side streets seemed to be gradually melting into the earth from which they had come. Ben Harmony stepped down, regarding the *Enterprise* office the way an artistocrat would regard a tramp. He stripped the mitten off his right hand, walked up on the porch, and yanked the door open.

Shoumacher was in profile. He didn't seem to know Ben Harmony was there. He reached for the handle of the press.

"Hold it," Ben Harmony said.

Shoumacher looked around vaguely. When he saw Ben Harmony, his hands became still. "Sorry," he said. "I didn't hear you come in." His voice was polite; his hyperthyroid eyes were as wary as a cottontail rabbit's.

The place smelled of ink and whiskey. Shoumacher's pink face turned scarlet. "Well," he said, and gathered himself. "I've been hoping I'd run into you."

"To recover the knife you're sticking in my back?"

Shoumacher backed away from the press. "I suppose you've come gunning for me, have you?"

"There's no gun in my hand."

"There's a gun in your mind," Shoumacher said. "I won't fight you."

"You may have to."

Shoumacher shook his head. "One Rand more or less isn't worth dying for. And you *are* a Rand, aren't you?"

The pulse throbbed at Ben Harmony's throat. He shut the door behind him. "You're not a man, Shoumacher, you just look like one."

Shoumacher said nervously, "You're beginning to exhaust my patience. If you want a fight, you won't get any help from me, I've told you that. You'll have to do it all yourself. . . ." Shoumacher's voice ran down. Confronted by the glitter of Ben Harmony's eyes, he began to step backward. Ben Harmony loomed.

Clay found Dinwiddie in the freight yard office. Dinwiddie had a bottle of whiskey before him. He made a gesture. "Come in—come in. I've been sitting here feeling rather old and neglected." He talked too brightly. He peered forward, as if the light were bad. "Your face looks like it could hold a three-day rain. You must have digested the news. Feeling sorry for yourself, are you?"

"No."

"No? You're putting on a pretty good imitation of it."

Clay could never make himself come to terms with his contradictory feelings about Dinwiddie. In spite of every disagreeable thing he knew about Dinwiddie, he tended to like the man.

Dinwiddie said, "Look, I've been kicking myself ever since Shoumacher blurted it out. It was my fault."

"How?"

"Maybe I could have stopped him."

"He was telling the truth, wasn't he?"

"I guess he was. But he had no right to spring it like that. He's after your father. He only tangled with you because you were handy. I wish I'd had the nerve to shut his mouth."

Clay's face was set. He was thinking about how to phrase what he wanted to say. Dinwiddie said, "As God is my witness, I just didn't think. If I had, I'd have stopped him somehow. I don't think I'll forget it if I live to be a thousand years old."

"You didn't do anything, Dinwiddie."

"That's easy for you to say."

"Your judgment's all tangled up in that booze. Look, if you want to make amends so bad, you can do something for me."

"Name it."

"Just don't say anything about what happened this morning. Don't tell anybody about Ben being my half brother."

"It'll be in the paper tonight."

"Maybe it won't," Clay said.

Dinwiddie shook his head solemnly. "You'll never talk him out of it. You can't beat him."

"You can't always go by that."

Dinwiddie said, "All right, I'll keep mum. I hope you know what you're doing."

"So do I."

His father and mother, knowing the truth about Ben Harmony, had concealed it deliberately. They had denied Ben his birthright. Clay stood on the porch of the Occidental, bitterly staring at the ludicrous shape of the courthouse; he was ready to lurch inside the saloon when a rising babble of voices drew his attention toward the lower end of the street.

Clyde Littlejack was waddling fast toward the newspaper office, where streamers of smoke issued from the windows and whipped away in the wind. Littlejack, yelling hoarsely, broke into a shambling run. A knot of men approached cautiously from the far side of the street, talking loudly with gestures; someone ran out of Feldman's dry goods store with half a dozen clattering pails. The cry, *"Fire!"* echoed along Partridge Street.

Clay saw his father erupt running from the courthouse, Harry Greiff right on his heels and Colonel McAffee following shortly. Clay dropped off the Occidental stoop and hesitated. Afraid of what he might find, he hung back; his father came along, polished black boots pumping, and yelled at him to come on. Clay fell in and ran with them.

The street filled with people. Splashing buckets of water passed through the crowd; Littlejack and some others stood outside the *Enterprise* office, waiting to receive the water pails. Littlejack smashed in several panes, reached for a bucket and flung water through to the inside.

Smoke got in Clay's nose and made him sneeze. He

rammed into the crowd behind Harry Greiff. Someone thrust a bucket at him. Water splashed cold down his trousers. He passed the bucket on to the next man and pressed through the brigade line. The church bell began to bang insistently.

Clay plunged through to the boardwalk and got up on his toes, blinked back smoke, and sought out Ben Harmony. Ben's face was nowhere visible in the crowd. Voices caromed against Clay's ears. Red-blue flames tongued out through the windows of the newspaper office, fed by the rushing cold wind, driving Littlejack and the others back. Littlejack was bellowing.

At the head of the street the volunteer fire engine appeared, dragged by hand by eight or ten men; it came rocking forward, brilliant red. Clay's father was speaking deliberately, making himself heard by those close to him. Gradually the sheriff achieved organization: the bucket brigade became orderly, passing buckets to and from the fire; a lane opened up in the crowd to let the fire engine through, and Littlejack climbed up on one end of the pump handle. Three men took the other end and sawed up and down. A chain of men dragged out the hose, uncoiling it along the earth. Droplets of water dribbled from the spout; a spurt ran out across the street; and then the pump pressure took hold and the heavy stream sprayed from the nozzle, almost driving it out of Harry Greiff's hands.

The thick fountain played across the front of the *Enterprise* building. Smoke-stung and coughing, Clay stood in the bucket line and passed pails back and forth across his belly. He couldn't find Ben Harmony anywhere. He had time to see Shoumacher's wife, Ethel, running forward along the far sidewalk with her skirts lifted. She uttered a strangling cry.

Dinwiddie hurried along behind her, impossible to mistake in his stovepipe hat, puffing like a steam engine. Across the street a window banged up in its sash and two ladies put their heads out. Their hands fluttered. Clay gave up looking for Ben Harmony and sought Shoumacher's face in the crowd, and when he could not find it, he felt the taste of fear like dry brass on his tongue.

Harry Greiff with both feet braced was aiming his fire hose as if the *Enterprise* were some enormous urinal. With Littlejack's muscle ramming the pump, the flow shot powerfully across an arc: it drove the flames back from the storefront and Harry Greiff climbed onto the boardwalk, dragging the hose. Clay saw him aim the nozzle through the broken windows, covering a pattern like a farmer scattering seed, rolling the fire back. Flames burst through the roof, and the wind whipped them into an earsplitting roar: smoke rolled into the street in fast-moving clouds.

Colonel McAffee was standing on an overturned bucket, trying to make himself heard, puncutating his talk with wild swings of his pudgy arms. Clay couldn't hear his words.

Harry Greiff got a look inside while he thrust the nozzle into the windows. He turned his head and bawled. The sheriff ran up beside him and flung an arm across his face, arrested by the heat but trying to see into the burning office. Clay saw him wheel back and snatch a bucket of water from a man in the brigade line. The sheriff ripped off his coat and plunged it in a wad into the bucket, soaking it through. He draped the coat over his head, strode to the door, and disappeared into the whirling smoke.

Clay dropped a bucket. It missed his foot by an inch. He ran forward—someone behind him exploded into angry bellows. He leaped onto the porch and grabbed Harry Greiff by the sleeve. Greiff thrust him back. Clay could hear his father coughing; he had a swirling vision of his father weaving through the flames, searching. Greiff covered the sheriff with a rain of hose water. Clay opened his mouth to speak; he didn't get anything said. He kicked the door back, buried his face in the crook of his arm, and tried to get inside. The heat drove him back.

Someone grabbed him roughly. "Stay out of there, you damn fool." It was Dinwiddie. Somewhere he had lost his stovepipe hat. His face was slack with fear; he trembled heavily. "What in God's name do you think you're doing?"

"Get him out of there," Clay mumbled.

"I brought this on us all," Dinwiddie said, hollow and without reasoning. His words dissolved into the roar of the fire.

Clay's father came backing out, hunched. A corner of his coat smoldered. He seemed to be dragging something. Greiff turned the hose and drenched the sheriff from head to foot. Clay saw his father nod gratitude. The sheriff backed onto the walk, dragging a charred body by both arms. Greiff doused the body. Most of the clothes were gone; the flesh was seared black.

"Ben," Clay said. Smoke in his lungs made him double over.

"No," Dinwiddie said in his ear. "It's Phil Shoumacher—look for yourself."

The sheriff dragged Shoumacher to the edge of the walk. Shoumacher slid down into the street. His head was bent far over to one side. He was plainly dead, as dead as a man could get; he looked like a corpse that had been rotting a hundred years.

Dinwiddie turned around like a sleepwalker and went away.

The sheriff flung his coat away. His face and hair were black with ash. He coughed his lungs clean and stood up straight. "Snap out of it, all of you. Fight this fire."

Clay saw Harry Greiff clamp down with his will on his feelings. Greiff turned the hose into the building. The sheriff said, "Never mind that. Wet the buildings next door."

Smoke tickled Clay into a spasm of coughing. Men ran past him with buckets and threw water as high as they could onto the roofs of the adjacent stores. At that moment the front wall of the *Enterprise* tilted inward slowly and collapsed in pieces. Flaming cinders shot through the smoke. Buckets clattered: men threw their arms before their faces. Embers crackled around Clay's feet. His father placed both palms against Clay's chest and thrust him backward. He tumbled off the boardwalk, aware suddenly that his eyebrows were singed and smoldering. He scrubbed them with his palms.

Someone had relieved Littlejack at the pump. Littlejack came shouldering through the smoke, puffing and wheezing. He brushed past Clay and found the sheriff. Clay heard his angry talk.

"You better find that nigger of yours, Farris, and slug the bastard in jail. I seen him come out of this place just before the fire started and whip up his horse like as if he had sixteen devils on his black tail."

Dinwiddie appeared, still hatless. He walked by the sheriff without seeing him. Dinwiddie knelt by the charred corpse and laid copper pennies on Shoumacher's eyelids. Narrow as a plank, Dinwiddie began to get to his feet; then he reached out and picked up something that glittered.

Dinwiddie came to Clay, holding out the bit of metal. He said in a dull tone, "Funny. His watch is still ticking, but not him. Christ, I hate this country. It kills everyone."

Chapter 17

SCATTERED embers glowed, stirred fretfully by the wind. Half a block of buildings lay razed under the afternoon sky. Men wandered vaguely through the wreckage. The sheriff summoned his horse and walked to the courthouse to gather his guns. When he came outside, armed to the teeth, Harry Greiff was waiting with two saddled horses. The sheriff never did get mounted; he was three strides from his horse when Ben Harmony rode into town.

He rode the length of Partridge Street, up to the courthouse, not looking back at the crowd he accumulated. It started by twos and threes at the edge of town and multiplied as Ben Harmony progressed down the thoroughfare. It swelled and surged behind his plodding horse. Clyde Littlejack was in the lead. Ben Harmony reached the courthouse and sat on his horse looking down at the sheriff.

"You're not dead," Farris Rand said.

"If I am, somebody forgot to burry me."

When Ben Harmony dismounted, the sheriff and Harry Greiff fixed themselves to him. Greiff brought him up on the walk. "Don't get notions," Ben Harmony said, and yanked his sleeve out of Greiff's grip. The sheriff came up, and they stood in a little knot, ringed by the crowd.

Greiff lifted his voice. "Would you be givin' us a bit of room here, boys?"

The mass of people crowded the square, hundreds of them, filling up the walks, climbing balconies and standing on wagons for a better view. Littlejack's eyewitness story had wasted no time making the rounds. The proud citizens of Ocotillo pressed out of open doors and windows, shifting and milling. A commotion rippled; a shout rang along the street. It gathered in a well of voices. On the edge of it, trying to push through, Clay got swept up in the surge. His eyes widened and he took a step back, against the corner of the court-house. A glimpse of a cowboy's contorted face struck rage into him.

Ben Harmony was pressed back in the doorway, defiantly trying to stare them all down at once. Greiff opened the door and thrust him through. Clay grunted and heaved; he made his way painfully along the base of the wall to the steps, used his elbows and shoulders to get through, and went up. His father let him pass. There was a bright gleam in his father's eyes. Clay wheeled inside with him. They had to lean together against the door to close it on the crush of men.

"Upstairs," his father grunted. He gave Ben Harmony a shove.

Their quick footfalls echoed up the staircase. Ben Harmony balked at the head of the stairs. Harry Greiff said, "I'd stay friendly, young fellow." Greiff stepped across the landing and opened the office door.

They went inside. The sheriff put down his guns. "You busted his neck, Ben. He's dead."

"Who says I was the one?" Ben Harmony said.

"Littlejack."

"Sure. He'd say anything that'd get me strung up to dry in the sun."

"You deny it?"

"I'm not talking," Ben Harmony said, "and that's all."

The sheriff's soot-blackened head moved back and forth. "This day has been a long time coming, hasn't it, Ben?"

At the vanguard came trumpeter and drummer. It was Dinwiddie who led the saddled, riderless horse with Shoumacher's hat and shoes tied behind a large wreath of greens. Behind Shoumacher's horse came the brass-railed gleaming black hearse drawn by six black horses; through the glass sides of the hearse could be seen Philip Shoumacher's diamond willow casket. Shoumacher was going out in style.

The widow, veiled in black, walked behind the hearse. The populace, suitably subdued, followed in a slow, shuffling procession. It was a brittle gray morning. Trumpet and drum played the thin, slow march. In an alley mouth a drifter sat on his horse, hat across his chest, and watched with patient resignation; all the saloons were closed.

Clay marched with his father, flanked by a body of men in black suits. They walked out of town up the hill. Clay stood near the open grave, not looking Shoumacher's widow in the face.

According to custom, the sermon took up a good deal of the morning. The widow leaned on Dinwiddie's arm. On occasional Sunday afternoons the preacher had been to supper at Sheriff Rand's house, and Clay had found him tedious then; he found him equally tedious now. The preacher was a florid, fat little man with a baritone monotone and a tendency to harangue. He launched into a dogged summary of the damnations and blessings waiting beyond the grave, the sins and virtues of mortal men, the adjurings of prophets, and the value in eating unleavened bread. For one space of at least thirty minutes he did not once mention the deceased. Cold winds battered the hill and set spectators to shifting from foot to foot. Finally Philip X. Shoumacher was laid to rest, the widow sprinkled the coffin with cold dry earth, and the crowd moved back into Ocotillo, walking much more briskly than before.

Little groups broke off to find their way home. Clay heard someone say, "He was a hated man. Too many people hated his guts. Hadn't been the nigger, somebody else would've killed him. Or maybe he'd have poisoned himself on his own bile."

"Keep your stupid voice down, Larry. You want the widow to hear you?"

Clay stepped out of the crowd and climbed the gun shop porch to let them go by. He saw his parents turning up Holliday Street. His father held his mother's arm and kept talking; his mother kept shaking her head in disagreement.

They walked out of sight. Clay thought about going home; there would be a fight if he did. He felt ready to explode. His loyalties were confused, tangled by his father's refusal to acknowledge his firstborn son and by Ben Harmony's stubborn muteness.

He went down to the courthouse. For a while he stood outside, bending his head back to look at the tilted gables and the barred windows. Ben Harmony's cell was behind one of them. *My brother Ben.* Clay was lonely and unsure. He went inside, graven-faced, and climbed the stairs.

Harry Greiff said, "Maybe you can talk to him."

"Me? What about?"

"He won't even talk to a lawyer."

"What the hell," Clay said. "Can I go on back?"

"Sure." Greiff waved a hand toward the cell block door. "How was the funeral?"

"It was a barrel of laughs," Clay said gloomily, and went out the side door of the office into the cell corridor.

The first cell belonged to Billy Cordell. Billy was waiting for his trial; he had been held over. Clay didn't glance inside; he went on by, back to the far end of the hall. The last cell was Ben's.

Ben Harmony gave his sour face one look. "Lose something, Chico?"

Clay said, "I don't get you. Harry says you won't see a lawyer."

"What lawyer can I see? McAffee?" Ben waved his hands. "Chico, the verdict was written down the day I got born. I don't need a lawyer to tell me that. Quit looking at me with those Sunday-go-to-church eyes. I'm no different from what I was yesterday."

"Did you kill him, Ben?"

Ben Harmony studied him through the bars. "You want me to be guilty, don't you?"

"If you didn't do it, then who did?"

"Maybe he did it himself. Maybe he fell down and busted his neck and knocked over the lamp."

"He didn't pie the type himself," Clay said. "It was scattered all over the floor in there, even before the walls caved in."

"No," Ben Harmony agreed. "I did that."

"To keep the newspaper from getting printed. Did you burn the place down just to make sure?"

"Chico, you can draw your own conclusions."

Clay said, "I'm trying awful hard to believe in you. Can't you give me a little help?"

"Not a bit," said Ben Harmony. "But you can give me a little help. Drop out to the ranch and pick up my war bag. I'm particular about wearing a clean shirt every day."

Clay wrapped his fists around the bars. "Do I have to tell you what the sentence will be if they find you guilty?"

"I've seen a man hang before. Flaps like a dead fish on a hook."

"Then will you, for God's sake, see a lawyer?"

Ben came forward, near enough to touch him, but he kept his hands in his pockets. "Listen, Chico, I want you to look at my face. What do you see? I'm not white, and I'm not going to be white, no matter how hard I try. In this town or any other town I know, I'll get a trial. A trial just like a dog gives a flea. Now quit throwing lawyers at me, all right? The lawyer hasn't been born who can paint me white."

Clay yelled at him. "You won't even fight for your rights, will you? You're my brother, Ben. You're his son."

"Not until he says I am," Ben Harmony breathed. "Now go away, Chico. You don't amuse me anymore."

Susan Rand wrapped herself in a shawl and sat before the fire. The sheriff chewed a cigar to shreds. His wife said, "I went to church before the funeral. To pray for Ben Harmony. But I'm not sure I wasn't praying for myself. You're not just bringing it down on your own head—you'll destroy us all. Why didn't you take him in? Why didn't you give him what's his?"

"You wouldn't understand," Farris Rand said.

"If I wouldn't understand, who would?" Her busy fingers mangled the ends of the shawl. "If I were Ben Harmony, I'd have made you crawl."

"You're not Ben," he said.

"I'd squeeze you. I'd make you hurt, the way he must be hurting now."

"Don't you think I've done a fair job of that myself?"

"Nothing to what ought to be done to you," she said. The room was gray and cold. "You!" She had to stop and start again. "For what you've done to Ben Harmony, Farris, there's no one on this earth who'll forgive you."

"I did what had to be done. Ben knows that."

"Nothing of the kind!"

"Nobody can turn black into white, Susan."

"Nobody asked you to," she answered. "But if you'd been a man, you'd have given him his due."

"Do you think I'm the only white man on earth who's

fathered a black child? Do you think Ben Harmony is the only one ever born?" The sheriff's massive head bowed. "Susan, do you want me to put on sackcloth and ashes for the rest of my life because I planted one seed?"

"Ask Ben, not me. And you should have asked him a long time ago." Her hands were shaking so much she couldn't get a proper grip on the crumpled shawl; she flung it away in despair. "Is there any doubt of his guilt?"

"Depends on what you mean by guilt. Shoumacher got what he deserved. I doubt it will get Ben in any trouble with the Almighty. Sooner or later we've all got to dirty our hands a little. I'm not convinced Ben did the murder, but if he did, he has no reason to regret it."

"No reason to regret that he'll hang?"

"That," said the sheriff, "is justice."

"Justice," she said. "Justice? Is that what it is? What about mercy, then—or did mercy die on the cross?"

"That's a matter for the judge, not for me. I'm only a sheriff."

She said, "The body wears the badge, not the soul. Farris, you heard what Clay said last night. How can you ignore it? Ben went to Shoumacher's place to stop him from printing evidence that would have ruined your life in this town. If you'd acknowledged that Ben was your son when he first came here, none of this would have happened. Shoumacher would have had no weapon against you. You murdered Shoumacher, Farris."

"Don't say that too often," he droned. "And once more will be too often."

"Hate. That's the only thing that warms you anymore, isn't it?"

"Grab yourself some sense. Sometimes you're a foolish woman, Susan. You refuse to face the fact that life is real."

"You never listen, do you?"

The sheriff went to his office. He said to Harry Greiff, "Does McAffee still want to talk to Ben?"

"I reckon."

"Ask him to come in, then."

Greiff went out. His boots banged down the hall toward McAffee's office. The sheriff bit off the tip of a cigar and walked through the side door into the cell block. He looked

into the first cell. Billy Cordell was waving flies away from
his injured leg. Dr. Smyley was there; the cell door stood
open. Smyley snipped out a fresh bandage and said to Cordell, "The first time I ever laid eyes on you, I knew you'd be
one of those hell-raisers who had to do everything the hard
way."

"Give me another snort of that medicine," Billy Cordell
said. "Hello, Farris."

"How're you making it, old friend?"

Billy Cordell's emaciated features were dignified by pain.
He said, "This idiot sawbones says I ain't going to pull
through. I reckon you've killed me, Farris."

The sheriff nodded. "I guess I have."

"They tell me it hurts like hell to die."

"That's not true," the doctor said sharply.

Billy Cordell raised his head. "How the hell would you
know? You ever tried it?" His head sagged back onto the
cot. "Goddam it, Farris, I still want to grab the world by the
tail and spin it around."

The doctor buckled his bag shut and stood up. "Try to get
some sleep now."

"Doctor, I won't have to try." Billy Cordell held out his
hand, palm up. "Look there, Farris. Nothin' left but a fistful
of lost dreams. Thirty years I've spent prowling the hills, and
seems to me I never yet walked down a mountain. They all
go the same way—up. One way to get to heaven, I guess.
That country's full of bones that went out hunting for gold,
but I never figured to be one of them. Hey, Farris?"

"Yes?"

"My belly feels like my throat's been cut."

"I'll get you something to eat," the sheriff said.

"Yeah. You do that."

The sheriff followed Smyley back into the office. When he
shut the door, Farris Rand said, "Damn it, Emmett, I shot
him in the leg on purpose. What's all this caterwauling about
dying?"

"That leg's crawling with death," Smyley said. "Nothing I
can do about it. Nothing anybody can do. I could saw it off
at the hip and give him a few extra weeks, but he won't let
me do that. I'm kind of inclined to agree with him."

"I never wanted this on my conscience."

"I'm glad you can't see yourself," Smyley said. "I can look

right through you and see your heart break. It isn't your fault, Farris. Don't search your soul. Billy's dying because he couldn't change when the country changed."

At the door the doctor added softly, "I hope you don't make the same mistake, Farris."

He went out, leaving the door open to admit Harry Greiff. Greiff came in with Colonel McAffee in tow. The sheriff said, "Get a meal for Billy Cordell, will you?"

"He just ate a couple hours ago."

"Get it anyway," Farris Rand said. "Get him anything he wants and put it on my private bill."

"Sure," Greiff said, and went.

Colonel McAffee leaned on his walking stick. His nose, bloated and veined, was a beacon preceding him. He blinked with satisfaction. "Go right on mollycoddling the old bastard, Farris. You're playing right into my hands. Election in eleven days, you know."

"Is that what you wanted to see me about?"

"There's no duck like a sitting duck," the colonel said. "But no. Not that. I came to see the Nigra."

"What for?"

"My duty, you know. I'm the only qualified defense lawyer in town."

"You'd defend him?" the sheriff asked.

"I'll be honest with you. I've got no use for him, no use at-tall. But I'm a fair man. The Nigra's got to have a just trial. To vindicate what Shoumacher stood for. Law and order, Farris. Not your Old Testament kind, but the real animal."

The sheriff said, "You won't win any votes by defending him."

McAffee smiled. "Won't come to trial until after the election, will it, now?"

The sheriff stepped to the door. "All right. Come on."

"Can I see him alone, please?"

"First we'll find out if he wants to talk to you."

They went back along the corridor. The sheriff glanced into Billy Cordell's cell and kept right on going.

McAffee banged his walking stick on the bars of Ben Harmony's cell. "Come over here."

Ben Harmony was on the cot, hands laced behind his

head. "I like it fine right here." He had looked at McAffee just once.

McAffee said, "I hear you killed Philip Shoumacher. Is that right?"

"What do you think?"

"How did it feel?"

Ben Harmony said, "He didn't say."

"Have you been apprised of your rights?"

Ben Harmony just laughed. McAffee's belly poked against the bars. "They'll indict you, you know. And no prosecutor ever indicts a man unless he expects to convict him. You'll need a defense attorney."

Yawning, Ben Harmony patted his lips.

McAffee said, "Do you know what your future looks like, boy?"

Ben Harmony turned his head to one side to look at him. "Do *you* know what the future looks like? What do you use—tea leaves or a crystal ball?"

"Let's try cards, boy. Let's put them face up on the table. If I'm to defend you, I've got to know the facts."

"Forget it."

"You want to die, don't you? Or am I mistaken?"

"Your mistake could be in asking," Ben Harmony said. He seemed more indifferent than annoyed.

"Maybe you don't know this, boy. A lawyer doesn't have to believe in his client in order to defend him. I can help you."

"Why?"

"Because justice will be on trial. I intend to see you're treated fairly."

"I'll be treated fair," Ben Harmony said. "I'll be sentenced fair and hanged fair. You can draw lots for my corpse, and that'll be fair, too."

He looked straight at Farris Rand.

McAffee turned. He hawked and snorted. "Black, red, or white, he's guilty, Farris. The Emancipation Proclamation doesn't give them the license to commit murder." McAffee clumped out of the corridor.

The sheriff remained at Ben Harmony's cell. "You should have taken him up on it."

"I don't want any lawyers, old man."

"Why not?"

Ben Harmony sat up and put his feet on the floor. "You know what'll happen if they start a gum fight in court. Somebody will get the bright idea to put Dinwiddie on the stand. Dinwiddie knew all about it. Is that what you want?"

"I never expected anything else," Farris Rand said.

"Then you're not thinking straight. All you've got to do is let Clyde Littlejack and the rest of them get a little drunk. Just stand aside and let them drag me out and lynch me. Dinwiddie will keep his mouth shut, and you'll be clear of it—clear of me. That's what you want, isn't it?"

The sheriff locked glances with him. "Are you trying to make it a question of conscience, Ben?"

"Yours or mine?"

"Because if you are, I won't have it. McAffee was right. If you're guilty, you'll hang, and nothing you or Dinwiddie can say will stop it."

"And if I'm not guilty?" Ben Harmony said. His voice was dust-dry.

"I haven't heard you say you were."

"Name one man who'd believe me if I did say it."

"I might," the sheriff said.

"Might. Not good enough, old man."

"Try me." The sheriff grasped the bars. "Try me, boy."

When the sheriff left the courthouse, he went directly to Dinwiddie's freight yards. He found Dinwiddie forted up in his office with a bottle. Dinwiddie regarded him owlishly. "Got some more money to give back to me?"

"Not this time," the sheriff said. "I'd like a minute of your time."

"Time," said Dinwiddie. "At my back I hear time's winged chariot hurrying near. Something like that, wasn't it? There's a glass someplace in that mess on the rolltop. Help yourself to a drink."

"Not right now. Shoumacher told you certain things about me before he died."

"You and your son," Dinwiddie said. "Ben Harmony."

"My son Clay," the sheriff said, "had a talk with you."

"That was several years ago. I seem to recall it vaguely." Dinwiddie hoisted the bottle to his lips. His face was lobster red.

Farris Rand said, "I don't intend to hold you to any

promises you may have made. When Ben Harmony goes on trial, I expect you to make yourself available as a witness, and I expect you to testify truthfully."

Dinwiddie blinked. He coughed on the whiskey, put the bottle down, and searched for a handkerchief to wipe the dribble on his chin. Finally he blotted it with his sleeve. "Generous," he said. "This may strike you as odd, but for the first time I find it in my power to do something worthwhile for a fellow human being. It's just my misfortune the human being in question has to be you, Farris. But that's the way it turned out. Life is an irony devoutly to be scorned. Be that as it may, I intend to keep my lips sealed upon the word that you are that black man's father. Phil got what was coming to him, and if your son was the instrument of it, then it's his hard luck. But I can't take it on myself to show the world the skeleton in your closet. If you want that done, you'll have to do it yourself."

"Will you testify?" the sheriff insisted.

"Who knows? I may drink myself to death before then." Dinwiddie lifted the bottle and waved it. "So long, Farris. Hard luck to you."

The sheriff stopped at the Widow Shoumacher's house. From the porch he could hear the sound of the woman's choked sobbing. The preacher came out onto the porch, lifting his hat to his head; he stopped and said, "If I were you, Sheriff, I'd go on about my business and leave her to do her grieving in peace." The preacher trotted down the steps and walked away.

Farris Rand raised his heavy silver head. He rapped with his knuckles and went inside.

Ethel Shoumacher recognized him through her tears. She wiped her face. "I often thought about him dying. He wasn't well, you know. I didn't think I'd care at all."

The sheriff said, "I am sorry, ma'am."

"Don't be. There's nothing that can touch him now."

"He gave me something to keep for you," the sheriff said. He placed an envelope on the table before her. The woman sat up on the divan, looked at Rand and at the envelope.

It made her laugh a little. "You're lying, Sheriff. Of all the men he'd have given that to, you'd have been the last. Thank you, but no."

She laughed again, with tears close behind.

The sheriff said, "He couldn't trust himself not to spend it. It wasn't much of a provision for you. He lost money on the newspaper, you know."

"I know. And the rest went into bottles. But I can't accept your money."

"He left it to you. Don't make me break the promise I made him."

She broke down. "I'm not proud enough to refuse you again. I'm afraid I do need it. If it helps your conscience, then God reward you, Sheriff."

The sheriff went outside quickly. She had surprised him; her sadness had been genuine.

A door flew open next door, as if the woman had been leaning against it with her ear to the wood. She came across the lawn. Wordlessly, the sheriff stepped aside. The woman rushed into the house. The sheriff jammed his hat down on his head and went away.

Chapter 18

THE wedge Ben Harmony had driven into Ocotillo divided the town into opposing camps of unequal proportions. Colonel McAffee, whose conscience had bitten him when he wasn't looking, brought his walking stick and a bottle of John Vale into the sheriff's office and said, "I suppose you've heard what Clyde's up to."

"I have."

"He ought to be silenced. Before he whips them up into a mob."

"I don't think there'll be any lynching," said the sheriff.

"Feelings are running pretty high. The argument got so bad last night at Dinwiddie's house that his wife refused to feed him."

"I know. I saw him drinking his supper in the Occidental."

McAffee said in a sour voice, "The Nigra is innocent until proved guilty. Equal justice under law. That's what Shoumacher fought for. Farris, it's a very strange turn of events that puts you and me on the same side of this."

"For you," the sheriff agreed, "it's a political red-hot poker."

"I'd be smart to drop it before it burns my hand to cinders, wouldn't I?" He uncorked his bottle. "Can't have the audacity to disagree with the moral codes of five thousand years, though. Right's right. It's open and shut."

"Don't you mean black and white?"

"Are you going to give me an argument, Farris?"

"Do you want one?" The sheriff sank his teeth in a cigar. "Your nose is out of joint. What do you want of me?"

McAffee said, "You wanted to break Phil Shoumacher, because he wanted to break you. The Nigra's crime played right into your hands. That's why you're treating him like a house guest instead of a prisoner. Fight scum long enough and you become scum yourself. Farris, you're not real anymore, you're just playing the part of sheriff. You've let things get the better of you. You look terrible. You need a rest. Have you thought of retiring?"

The sheriff waggled his hand toward the door. "I won't dignify that with an answer."

"I'm quite serious."

"You're fat, McAffee. Where you sit and where you think."

"And you are *not* a law unto yourself."

"You're reaching for any stick you can use to beat a dead horse," the sheriff said. "I tolerate you only because you've had the decency to sacrifice your ambition for the benefit of a principle, but it doesn't make me feel charitable. You've lost the election. Don't carp at me on that account. I've listened to your bumbling arguments and I—"

"You've listened very carefully," McAffee cut in, "to every word you've had to say. You've let personal consideration interfere with the job. It's time you turned in your badge."

"Nobody pensions me off," the sheriff said. "McAffee, your world and your nose end at the same place. Have you ever stopped to think what would happen to you if you had the bad luck to become sheriff here? The toughs would have your guts for guitar strings."

Clay stayed in the Occidental long enough to listen to the timbre of the talk; afterward he went to McAffee's house. The colonel, he knew, was still downtown drinking. Lavender was home alone.

Her red hair hung loose and heavy around her face. She had one look at Clay's expression and her mouth pinched at the corners. She reached for his hand—it was ice-cold—and drew him into the dining room. "You haven't eaten."

"Forgot, I guess."

"I'll fix something. Lay off your things."

He wouldn't release her hand. He said, "We don't judge each other, do we? We love each other."

"What is it, Clay? What's wrong?"

He had not confided in her, not up to now. He searched for words. She put a finger to his lips and said, "Don't you know that I love you beyond belief?"

He said, "There's something I haven't told you." His mouth worked, and he wrapped both hands around hers. Her eyes were very big. He blurted, "Shoumacher was going to print a story that Ben Harmony's my half brother. My father's illegitimate son."

"But you—" she began, and stopped.

All he could do was shake his head. "Forgive me if you can."

"Forgive you?"

"I shouldn't have kept it from you."

All through the meal she didn't speak. Once she started to say something; her voice changed and she said, "You don't ever have to tell me anything just because you think you ought to." Clearly it was not what she had meant to say. She took both his hands and kissed them. "I love you so," she murmured.

They went into the parlor. Lavender turned down the lamps. "How do I look?"

"You look very special."

"I feel wicked, being alone in the house with you."

They sat on the divan, holding each other close and dreaming fretfully into the fire. She laid her head on his chest; she made him feel drunk. "Clay?"

"Yes, darling?"

"Do you know how grateful I am for your love?"

"We're both a little crazy," he said. He caressed her. A burst of wind howled past the house. He felt her begin to shake in his arms; he said, "What's wrong?"

"Nothing."

"Oh, I see. You cry every Friday night, that's all."

"Clay?"

"I love you," he said.

"Why did Ben do it?"

"Maybe he didn't do it. Nobody saw him do it. Maybe it was an accident."

"But if he did do it, why would he?"

His arm shifted, curling farther around her. He was continually surprised at how tiny her waist was. He said, "The story Shoumacher wanted to print was true. Ben is my half brother. If the story had come out, it would have ruined my father and mother, and you and me, too, I guess. Ben went down to the newspaper to stop Shoumacher from printing it. He did it for all of us. But I guess he did it for himself, too, because he wanted my father to accept him. I think maybe he wanted my father to love him."

"And now they'll hang him, won't they?"

"Maybe not. Nobody can prove he killed Shoumacher."

"It won't be proof that convicts him," Lavender said. "It will be his skin."

It surprised him that she should say that.

She said, "I grew up in the South. I know." She extricated herself gently from his arms and went to the fireplace to pick up the poker. "It's so cold in here." She stirred the fire and put the poker away, but she did not come back to him. She said, "Clay?"

"What?"

"If he is your brother, you ought to help him."

"How?"

"Save him," she said. She turned toward him, and he saw a shape to her face that he had never seen before. "Help him get away," she said. "Help him, Clay."

Clay found his father in the jail. The sheriff was sitting with Billy Cordell. The thin white moustache lay unevenly against Billy's seamed, unkempt face. He was lying on a blanket on the floor; he had always hated beds. His watery blue eyes had receded into their sockets. He was saying, "Food never tastes like food when you're scared," and he was shaking his head at the tray beside him. He did not seem aware that Clay had come into the cell.

He plucked at the sheriff's trouser cuff and said, "You shouldn't have let them make a town man out of you, Farris. Towns ain't natural. I'd stayed out of towns, I wouldn't be dying now. You put yourself in a town and nobody ever asks what side you're on. If you get in their way, they tear you apart. You listen to me, Farris, it's a big world, and they's something in it for everybody. You get on your horse and go where it's wild and where they ain't no towns to crowd you. You'll be all right then."

"Take it easy, Billy," said the sheriff.

"Look, get me a jug of red-eye, will you, Farris? I feel my time comin' on, and I always did want to go out dead drunk."

The sheriff glanced at Clay. "Get it."

Clay nodded and went over to the Occidental. He bought a jug of the cheapest raw corn Scotty had in stock; that was what Billy had always liked best. He hauled the jug back to the courthouse and up the steps.

When he went into the cell, Billy's eyes were closed. Clay said, "How is he?"

"Right now he's dead," said the sheriff. He got up from his knees and stripped the blanket off the mattress and spread it over Billy Cordell.

"So long, old friend," the sheriff said. "I hope the mountains are all downhill where you've gone."

He walked home with his father. His father went straight to the sideboard and poured himself a tumbler full of brandy.

Clay said, "I'm sorry about Billy."

"So am I."

"I kind of liked him."

"He sized up like a man," the sheriff said, and turned to the window. He lifted his glass in the general direction of the courthouse, making a private toast, and sipped off the surface. He put the glass down and put his arms akimbo, rising several times on his toes while staring out. It was a familiar gesture.

Clay said, "Look, what about Ben?"

"What about him?"

"I've been thinking."

"Don't think. It's not your strong point."

"I didn't ask for that," Clay said.

His father turned far enough to look at him. It struck Clay that he looked older.

Clay said, "He hasn't got a chance."

"Just so," his father said. He took his glass back to the sideboard and lifted the lid of the cigar box.

"He'll be railroaded right through. They'll hang him."

"It's possible."

"What do you mean, possible? You're the one that's always

telling me to face the truth. And the truth is, Ben will hang for sure."

His father's neat white teeth bit the tip off a cigar evenly. He extracted it with thumb and forefinger, scraped it off into the glass ash tray, and reached for a match. He said in a voice from which he withheld all feeling, "I expect he will, boy. What do you want me to do about that?"

Clay felt weight behind him. He turned to see his mother. He didn't know how long she had been there. She came into the room and stood, not quite near enough to touch him, watching his father with dark burned-out eyes. She seemed intent on extracting the essence of what was being said, as if squeezing the pulp of an orange she would not let go until the last drop of moisture dripped out.

Clay said, "Ben has no chance."

"And?"

"He's your son. My brother."

"I do know that, boy."

Susan Rand took one step forward and put her hand on Clay's shoulder. "Knowing what you know, you'll stand by him, Clay?" Her face shifted toward the sheriff. "Farris, you *must* let Ben escape."

"We've had that out before."

"You'd rather murder him, then?"

The sheriff said "Goddam all of you. I've got my duty to do."

She said, "That iron-bound sense of duty has made an animal out of you, Farris. I don't give a tinker's damn about your tin badge—I'm appealing to your heart, and so is Clay."

"The law is the law," he said dismally.

Clay said, "You can let him sneak out of town and make it look like he broke jail himself. Just give him a chance to get to Mexico."

"God!" the sheriff said. "And if I did that? I'd destroy us all and only make him into a fugitive for the rest of his life."

Clay said, "Right now he hasn't got any rest of his life."

Susan said, "Let him go, Farris. Let him go and I'll stay."

"What?" Clay asked.

Farris Rand shook his gray head. "Nothing you can say or do will change the law."

Clay felt the hard, steady pressure of his mother's hand on

his shoulder. His father tramped out of the room, gathering up his coat.

When the sheriff was gone, Clay's mother let her hand fall away. She said, "You're grown, Clay, and there's nothing more I can do for you. I told your father some time ago that unless he could change, I wouldn't stay with him. It was always a false dream, I know—no man is a caterpillar, nobody comes out of a cocoon and suddenly becomes a butterfly."

He had to swallow before he could answer; he said slowly, "You mean you're going to leave?"

"I've already packed."

"But—"

"No," she said. "It's done. I can't stay, Clay."

"Can I do anything?" he said; he felt stupid.

"Try to help Ben," she said. "Try as hard as you can."

Chapter 19

THE sky built up for a blow. A wind came rushing down the valley, picking up nebulas of fine silver dust. With a cigar teetering between his front teeth, the sheriff walked past the hotel and the bank and the tonsorial parlor. His face looked like a steel hatchet. His face registered no recognition when Hannah Early stopped him in front of Feldman's store.

She said, "If you ain't a sight."

"Cut it out, Hannah."

She said, "They ain't leaving you much, are they, Farris? Well, I seen it coming, and you would've too, if you'd kept your eyes open. You ever see a Mexican clean the rats out of his 'dobe? They throw a sidewinder rattlesnake inside the place and slam the door. Eats up all the rats. But nobody keeps the snake around for company afterwards. That's what they're doing to you, ain't it? I hear everybody's yellin' for you to resign. Why in hell couldn't you bend a little?"

He said, "I don't have to answer to you, Hannah."

"No, you don't. Might have to answer to somebody, though. Maybe yourself. For sure, your wife."

"Leave me alone," he growled. "I don't need your help."

"You sure don't, Farris. You don't need nobody's help. You need a goddam blind man's cane. Your wife just checked her bags in at the stage office. She's waiting for the railroad stage over there in the cafe."

His blank stare unsettled her. She stepped back. She said, "Maybe I should've kept my mouth shut. Better just to let her go, let her be a thousand miles away before you found out. They ain't left you much, have they? You poor son-of-a-bitch, Farris. You poor son-of-a-bitch."

He went toward the cafe; his feet dragged. Hannah watched him go inside. She drew her wrap around her shoulders. A cowboy was coming along the walk; Hannah put a smile on her face and winked at the cowboy.

"I told you I was leaving," Susan Rand said.

The sheriff spread his hands. "Where to?"

"I'd rather you didn't ask me."

He let himself down into a chair and faced her across the table. She said, "It's the emptiest hour in an empty life, Farris. I can't even cry."

"What about Clay?"

She only shook her head. Her hands were wrapped for warmth around a cup of coffee. She said, "I liked your face. It used to be a good face."

"I haven't changed."

"The world's full of fools, Farris, but you lead the parade."

He made an aimless gesture. "Just like that? Can't we talk?"

"Nothing to say."

He croaked at her. "Every street I walk down, I'll be looking for you."

"Don't. I won't be there. Farris, you've ruined so many lives I can't begin to count them. I'm too tired to wait any longer to see where it will end."

He reached toward her hand. "Can't you believe that I do have the remnants of a soul?"

"I think a little while ago I'd have wanted very much to believe you," she said. "But you're dead, Farris. You just haven't got the guts to lie down. Maybe Ben was wrong, but it doesn't mean that you were ever right. Oh, I apologize for my bitterness. But don't try to talk to me. Don't try to change my mind."

"Then you just want me to say goodbye? Here, like this?"

"I think we've said it." She gathered her handbag and wrap. "Clay will know where to find me. Please don't ask him to tell you."

Her eyes were distant, but they were unaccountably kind. She touched the edge of the table for support and stood up.

The sheriff got to his feet, clamping his jaws on his cigar. She slipped past him to the door. Moving like a mechanism, he followed her that far, but his glistening boots stopped in the doorway, and he put both hands against the jamb and watched her cross the street toward the depot. Her head lifted higher as she approached the waiting coach. Her step quickened. Clay was over there, helping the hostler stow Susan's bags in the coach boot. Clay turned to give her a hand up, and she stopped to talk to him. The sheriff could not hear their words. Once Clay's head turned, and his attention shifted toward the sheriff.

The cook strode out of the kitchen behind him. "Shut that damn door before we all freeze to death."

"Goodbye." *God be with you.* Clay watched the Abbott & Downing coach lean into the bend around the courthouse and buck across the dusty ruts. Pitching and clattering, it went out of sight, swaying on its leather springs. The driver's whoops slowly dissolved. Clay's glance lifted toward the barred gable windows of the courthouse.

He looked over his shoulder at the gray man on the cafe porch. He had lost not one but both of them. Not wanting to show tears, Clay walked to the livery stable to get his horse. He reached down a coiled rope, stiff with cold, and went back into the open corral. Ten or twelve horses milled sluggishly in the pen. Clay snaked out a loop in the rope and moved forward, dragging it behind him. His bay gelding shifted warily into the midst of the knot of horses. They all crowded up in a corner. Clay slapped a mare on the flank with his rope; the horses began to wheel fretfully around the corral, throwing up thin, cold dust and the smell of straw and manure. It made Clay sneeze. He dodged back and forth, working the bay into a corner where he got his loop over its head. He led it inside the stable, took down his bridle and lifted it. The bay tried to chop off his fingers when he pried the bit between its teeth. Clay smoothed the saddle blanket down, heaved the saddle in place, and planted his boot in the bay's belly to haul up the cinch.

He led it into the street, tossed one rein over, and mounted up.

His father stepped off the sidewalk and moved out, blocking Clay's path. "Where do you think you're going?"

It occurred to him that his father thought he intended to follow the stagecoach. Clay said, "Not far. I've got cows to look after, remember?"

His father grumbled something into his moustache. "I'm sure your mother has made some mistakes in her time, but nothing like this one."

"Maybe."

"Have supper with me tonight."

Clay tugged his hat down; his father looked up, awkward and small afoot. Clay said, "If I get back before sundown," and lifted the bay to a run, drumming out of town.

Thin drafts of air moved past Clay's face. The sky was occluded; there were no stars. Loose dust boiled around his horse's hooves. A lamp glimmered from a dairy-farm window, the only point of light visible. The chill made him close his fleece collar. He turned into a little-used road running along the back end of the farm.

The bay clipped along at a steady gait. He reached the back of town and made a wide circuit through the darkest streets; he tethered the bay in an alley opposite the side door of the courthouse.

Breathing shallowly through his mouth, he slipped to the courthouse and opened the side door with a key from his father's spare ring, always kept at home in the sheriff's rolltop desk. He shut the door silently and went up the dark back staircase.

In the office Harry Greiff was half asleep behind the desk. Clay passed the open door on tiptoe and padded into the cell corridor. A lantern, flickering on low oil, hung on a nail midway down the hall. He took it down and carried it back with him.

Ben Harmony was snoring softly on his cot. Clay unlocked the door and stood in the opening, softly speaking. "Ben?"

Ben Harmony sat up, squinting. He ground knuckles into his eye sockets. "Christ."

"You haven't got a whole lot of time," Clay said.

Ben came awake. "You're crazy, Chico."

"I kind of wish I was."

"You know what kind of trouble this will buy you?"

"It'll find me. It always seems to."

Ben Harmony stretched like a cat. "It isn't smart, Chico. If the old man ever gets his hands on you—"

"You want to sit there and argue or get out of here? There's a horse saddled in the alley across from the side door. Grub in the saddlebags and my mackinaw. I packed your guns and kit."

"Chico," said Ben Harmony, "fools are the only ones who get away with the impossible."

"Fools are the only ones who try." Clay stepped back. "You coming?"

"We could both end up in Boot Hill with dirt in our faces."

"You'll end up there if you don't go, that's for sure."

"Don't make any funeral arrangements until you're sure you've got a corpse," said Ben. The familiar grin flashed across his dark face. "All right, Chico. I reckon you only get one shot at life, and I'll take what's offered me. I figured somebody'd turn me loose."

"The old man?"

"Maybe that's what I was hoping. I've been lying here like Lazarus in his open grave, waiting for a savior to show up. I'm obliged to you, Chico."

"Head southeast to Oak Creek Canyon," Clay said. "That'll let you down through the Tonto Rim. From there if you're smart you'll cut hell-for-leather for the Mex border."

"And never be able to come back," Ben Harmony droned. "Then again, it's better than dead." He swung through the open door and gripped Clay, hard, on the arm. "I'm going to shake the world till it hollers uncle, Chico. Look me up sometime."

"Just take care," Clay murmured. He hung the lamp back on its nail. They slipped past the office door and down the back stairs. At the door Clay hesitated. "Ben."

"Yeah?"

"Good luck."

"What makes you think I ever needed luck?" Ben Harmony reached for Clay's hand and gripped it in the dark. Clay clamped it hard. Ben said, "Thank you, Chico."

"Make some sense out of your life," Clay said.

"Why should life make sense?" Ben chuckled sonorously. "Don't worry, I don't expect to be shaking hands with St. Peter for a while yet. Nervous, Chico?"

"No."

"You may not be, but your knees sure are. Where's that

horse? I'd better cut for it by myself. You stick here till I'm gone."

"Out the door and straight across to the alley."

"Let me take your hat."

Clay removed his hat and found Ben's hand in the dark "Here." He heard Ben latch the door open. A thin line of light appeared; Ben pressed his face against it and searched the street. Clay said, "Write me a letter to let me know you made it."

"I will." There was a quick squeeze of Ben's hand, and then he was through the door. Clay heard the light taps of his running footfalls. There was no outcry. A horse started up and trotted softly away. Clay raked fingers through his hair counted to one hundred, and stepped out through the door He rammed his hands into his coat pockets and strolled up the street.

He went into Hannah Early's and found Hannah at the bar. "Am I too young to buy you a drink?"

"Not if you're old enough to ask. Are you as lost as you look, Clay?"

He fixed his eyes on the drink that appeared before him Hannah said, "All people your age are unhappy sometimes Maybe if you're lucky it won't get worse when you get older."

Clay had difficulty raising the glass to his mouth. Hannah's big homely face shifted toward him. "Ain't a good idea to drink whiskey when things are going bad for you."

"Uh-huh."

"Do you want to talk about it?"

"Maybe," he said, "but not to you."

"You just want to sit there and listen to the tears run down your face."

"Hannah?"

"What, kid?"

"It's nothing but a puking trap, and that's the goddam truth."

"Relax, kid. You want to get loaded and sleep it off upstairs? Ain't nobody going to bother you. Want something to eat?"

"I thought you were strictly business."

"I am. Don't make no mistake, kid. I think a lot about money. I never sold myself cheap. Yeah, God made me as ugly as He could, and then He hit me in the face with a hammer. Well, then, I wish I'd been born beautiful, I wish somebody could have loved me—I was married once. To a gambler. All I ever did was play solitaire. He went out on the end of a rope."

He reached for the bottle to refill his glass. A girl came downstairs, giggling. Hannah put her palm on Clay's bottle and held it down. "You in a tight place, Clay?"

"Maybe."

"If you figure somebody aims to burn you at the stake, ain't no need to bring along your own jug of kerosene."

"I got to get out of here," Clay said. He left as abruptly as he had come. On the street he stared at the courthouse. It wouldn't be long before his father finished his last rounds of the night and made a bed check on the jail.

Chapter 20

THE sheriff's office filled with men. McAffee came in roaring, with Littlejack on his heels. Clay saw Dinwiddie go in after them. Clay went up the stairs two at a time; he rushed into the office in time to hear McAffee shout, "You're asking us to swallow a hell of a mouthful."

Littlejack said, "That deputy doodad don't guarantee you ain't a bald-faced liar, Harry."

"I can't help that," Harry Greiff said. "I didn't see nothing and I didn't hear nothing."

McAffee said, "He was let out with a key, Farris. Who else besides you has a key?"

"Nobody." The sheriff hooked down a rifle and went to his desk. "If you people will get out of the way, I'll be getting after the prisoner."

"There's a norther whipping up," Dinwiddie said. "You won't be likely to track anybody through a blizzard, Farris."

"He's gone for good," Littlejack growled. "And you let him loose."

"I did not let him loose," the sheriff said. Cords in his face made angry ripples. "He broke out of my jail. No man alive has ever escaped from my custody. Mr. Greiff, saddle our horses. I'll join you at the stable by the time you've got them ready."

Clay said, "Saddle mine, too, Harry."

His father glanced at him. "I don't want any amateur help, boy."

"I guess you've got it whether you want it or not."

168

"I think we'll all go," said McAffee. "Just to see that you do your duty—sheriff."

The sheriff said, "What is it you expect to win by that?"

"It's what we don't expect to lose," McAffee answered. "Clyde, go over with Harry and saddle enough horses for a posse. We'll need a pack horse and food for several days—Dinwiddie, that's your chore. Move, gentlemen."

The sheriff said, "I'm still running this office, McAffee. I don't need a pack of fat old men to slow me down."

"If any of us slows down, he'll fall out of the party," McAffee said. "You can't keep us from coming, Farris. You'd better accept that and quit wasting time with arguments."

"Then just stay out of my way." The sheriff was almost snarling. He yanked open a desk drawer and lifted out a box of rifle ammunition.

Clay went down to the stable with Harry Greiff. Littlejack cut across to his shop to get his gun. Harry Greiff got ropes down. "Ben Harmony's on the run from your pa's gun, Clay, and he knows what that means, for certain sure. I guess you can figure out for yourself what he'd likely do to anybody he thought was in his way."

Clay grunted.

"Keep your head down, then, and don't pet no stray dogs."

"All right, Harry."

The deputy turned up a lamp. "Me and your pa both, they're likely to tear off our hide in strips, we don't get Ben back."

"First we've got to catch him," said Clay.

"Saddle that buckskin. Got good legs. I'll get your pa's horse."

Clay was buckling up the back cinch when Littlejack lumbered inside and pitched in. Clay said, "You see the old man coming?"

"I'm coming," said Farris Rand, walking into the stable. "And I'll thank you not to call me the old man. All set, Mr. Greiff?"

"Just about, sir."

Farris Rand had a full gunnysack in one hand and his rifle in the other. It was the .45-90 long-range buffalo gun. Clay lifted his eyes from the long gun to his father's face. It was all closed up.

McAffee came marching in, with Lavender right behind him. "Clay?" she said.

Clay drew her aside into a stall. "Why'd you come here?"

"Didn't you want me to?"

"You'll catch cold without more clothes on."

"I'm all right," she said. She put on a smile. "Be careful—I like you alive."

"You haven't seen me dead. How do you know?"

"Don't joke about it."

He kissed her mouth. His father's voice brought him around. "Let's go, Mr. Greiff."

Clay came out of the stall. His father was mounted on his horse, stooping to clear the rafters. His coat collar was turned up, and lamplight glittered frostily on the surfaces of his eyes. "I want him found," the sheriff said, "and I want him taken apart." He reined his horse out of the stable.

Clay ran to his horse and got up. Lavender stood by the stall partition. He tried to smile at her. Harry Greiff rode by. "Ready, son?"

"I was born ready."

"Let's go, then."

The sheriff's voice came back from the street: "I'll give a hundred dollars to the man who finds his tracks."

Unaccountably, the storm held back. The third morning dawned bitter cold but bright. The previous day's thaw had hardened by night into a ground-crust that made hard footing for the horses. The progress of the posse had been slow and circuitous.

It was the waiting that put a ragged edge on Clay's nerves—the waiting and the not knowing whether Ben Harmony was going to make it. There were signs his horse had picked up a limp.

Clay lay against the cold earth with his cheek against the rifle stock. His father crouched behind him and talked under his breath. "He'll turn up from the creek in a minute. Always shoot on the rise, boy, and make sure of your shot. Never let them suffer."

The jackrabbit sat back at the creek and looked around. Light streamed through the oaks, its color very rich. Across the sun-spattered stream, the jack turned and humped up the steep bank as if on springs. Clay brought the rifle up and squeezed the trigger.

The jack lost its footing and fell sliding back to the creek. Its big hind legs drummed the earth.

"Good," his father said. "That'll provision us for another day."

His father's cheeks were barbed with a gray stubble; the untrimmed moustache was ragged and droopy. Clay got his feet under him and went unsteadily down to the stream. He unsheathed his knife, straightened out the rabbit carcass and set to skinning it. He watched his father prowl the hillside.

Clay's hand was weak with a tremor. He had been without sleep three days—eighty hours of riding, broken only by stops to swap horses at ranches and way stations.

Last night they had lost the spoor. Harry Greiff and the others had split away to circle for tracks. Clay was in no hurry to see them return. The knife worked bluntly; he ripped at the flesh with a weary curse. He saw everything through a drunken film that made nothing seem quite real.

His father came up. "You're doing a second-rate job of that."

"So tired I can't see straight. What do you expect?" Clay tossed hair out of his eyes. "We ought to lay over and get some rest."

"Ben's getting no more rest than we are. Don't you think you can do as well as he can?" His father hunkered down by him, a great rock of a man. "You may break, boy, but I won't let you quit."

"Why?"

"Don't beg, boy. Don't ever beg."

Sunlight made a clear stream of color, pearling the creek. Clay flashed his eyes to clear them and began to cut the meat in strips. His father helped knead salt into it. They packed it away and washed their hands in the creek. Racked with sores and half blind in a haze, Clay lay back, too tired to care about the vinegar smell of his own clothes.

His father's voice rode against him. "What made you think you could get away with it, boy?"

"What?"

"Do you know the penalty for abetting an escape?"

Clay kept his eyes closed. "You'll have to prove it first."

"And if I can't, that makes it right?"

Clay sat up. "Don't boil over so early or you'll run out of steam. I'm not in a mood to be preached at, not by you."

His father said, "Boy, you're not fit to shine my boots."

Blinking away the blaze of sunlight, Clay said, "To hell with you."

The posse rode through the forest. A rider swept in— Harry Greiff, his face glowing in the chill wind. "Picked up tracks going south. He's gone down through Oak Creek Canyon."

"Down the Rim," the sheriff said. "He's making a run for the border."

Littlejack said, "That'll be four days' ride, even if he had a fresh horse."

"And plenty of country to lose his tracks in between here and there," said Harry Greiff.

They rode ahead through a threadbare cover of snow that had trickled down during the noon hour. McAffee, shaking with fatigue, and Dinwiddie with his stovepipe hat crammed down over his ears, rode in the rear without complaint—and without any other sound. Clay was swaying in his saddle. Below, down the steep canyon, the creek made silver loops. The smell of pine resin whirled in streaky currents along this high rim that cut Arizona neatly in two. Bundled in his fleece coat and heavy mittens, Clay felt the bite in the air.

Harry Greiff said, "I come pret' near getting killed last winter on that trail. Tough enough summertimes. You get ice in the shadows, like to bust a horse's leg. Watch yourselves."

Without comment, Farris Rand put his horse over the rim. He leaned far back in the saddle to balance the horse.

Clay let his reins hang loose and gave the horse its head to follow Harry Greiff's. He clung to the saddle horn with both hands. His eyes slid shut—his mind sputtered and went out.

The horses jogged and jostled. Hairpin switchbacks took them down a two-thousand-foot drop off the Kaibab Plateau, down into desert country—the sprawling flat of monumental red stone mesas that stood on the chilly plain like forgotten remnants on an abandoned battlefield.

His father's voice weaved across his consciousness. "We'll change horses at Verde Crossing."

Greiff said, "He swapped for a palomino at Bannerman's. Everybody keep an eye out for it."

Four days of manhunting. Clay swam through the fog of sleeplessness. Small flakes of snow came riding the air currents.

Almost asleep, he heard his father say, "That's a palomino."

Clay brought it into focus then—the Verde Crossing station, half a mile across the butte-littered plain. Greiff said, "In the corral."

Colonel McAffee stirred his horse forward. He had a wadded towel under his rump. "Maybe the Nigra's still there."

"Maybe," said the sheriff. "We'll leave the horses here. But I may need them in a hurry. Mr. Greiff, you'll stay with them. If you see my signal, bring them along on the run."

"Yes, sir."

They dismounted, stiff in every joint. Clay tested his legs. He was weak behind the knees. They moved from brush to brush, manzanita and creosote and paloverde clumps, with the high dark clouds blacking out shadows. Keen to the possibility of ambush, the sheriff had his rifle in both hands. Clay heard him chamber a cartridge.

They reached a heavy line of greasewood. The sheriff said, "Scared, McAffee? All right, we're all scared—why shouldn't we be? But if Ben's in there, he's scared, too."

Clay watched the stir of cooksmoke from the way-station chimney. It lost itself in the rolling storm clouds. The station was a low box of a building, rooted firm in the emptiness. The ruts of the Gila Bend-Flagstaff coach road wound up out of the country to the southwest, whimsically called Horse Thief Basin, and continued north into the brush. It was a lonely stretch of bitter country where in the summer the only shade a man could find was his own shadow—and in the winter there was nothing to break a blizzard's wind.

The wind was rising.

"That's a palomino, all right," said Dinwiddie.

"Then cock your gun," the sheriff muttered. "You're blocking my view, Clay."

Clay moved aside to give him a clear field of fire. The sheriff sent his deep-voiced call rolling across the flats: "Horn. Sid Horn."

Grinding tensions set Clay's nerves afire. He rubbed one eye and then the other.

"Sid Horn. Come out where I can see you."

A voice roared from the station. "Who wants Sid Horn?"

"Sheriff Rand."

A tub-bellied man appeared in the door. "What you doing way out there? Come on in."

Dinwiddie said, "That gamy son-of-a-bitch."

Farris Rand said, "I'm looking for an escaped prisoner. Black skin. You got him inside there, Horn?"

"Nobody in here but me, Sheriff."

"Stand fast, then." In a lower voice the sheriff said, "Give us cover from here, you two. Clay, you'll come with me."

He stepped into the open, rifle across his chest. Clay walked out behind him. He had a firm grip on his gun, but it was not cocked.

Sid Horn was a big, loose man who sagged front and back. He had a thick brutal chin and a polished bald head. He stared at the sheriff with evident dislike. "Well?"

The sheriff said to Clay, "Check that horse, boy."

"I ain't seen no black-skin prisoner," said Horn.

Clay went to the corral. He kept swallowing. The palomino gelding trotted around the corral. Clay waited for it to come close so that he could read the brand. Then he went back to his father.

"Bannerman's brand, all right."

There was no point in lying about it.

His father said, "We'll have a look around inside, then."

"I told you, Sheriff, he ain't here." Sid Horn spoke with a prairie twang. He smiled falsely. "Ain't seen you since the last flash flood. Where you been keepin' yourself?"

"Where's my prisoner, Sid?"

"How in hell should I know?"

"He's been here."

"Has he?"

Farris Rand shouldered the fat man aside and went into the station. Startled, Clay lifted his rifle defensively. "Go in ahead of me, Mr. Horn."

"What the hell is this, anyway?" Horn shuffled inside ahead of Clay.

When they went in, the sheriff was coming from the back

of the place. "Not here," he said. "All right, Sid. Let's hear about it."

"Hear what?"

"I'm listening."

"I just don't recollect anybody being around this way lately, Sheriff."

The sheriff said, "You annoy me a little, Sid."

"Hell, you know my policy. I mind my own business. Ain't no other way to get along in these parts. If I was to start tellin' everything I know, my life wouldn't be worth cow dung."

"I'm overriding your policy, Sid. The prisoner broke out of my jail."

"Think of that."

"Where is he, Sid?"

"I don't know nothing now that I didn't know the last time you asked that question."

The sheriff had a poker stare. "You're a liar."

Horn said nervously, "I know. I've always been a liar."

The sheriff lunged forward. The barrel of the .45-90 sank three inches into Horn's belly. Horn backpedaled and grabbed his stomach, making sick noises. The sheriff said, "I want answers, and I'm beginning not to care how I get them."

Sid Horn's mouth opened and closed. "No."

The sheriff whacked him with a sharp, raking swipe of the rifle's front sight. It laid Horn's cheek open: he brought his hand away bloody.

"Goddam you, Sheriff. He was here. Swapped that palomino for a pinto gelding of mine."

"How much of a jump has he got?"

"Five, six hours maybe."

"All right. I'll forget you said anything."

"You do that."

"We'll trade you for fresh horses," the sheriff said. "Return exchange on our way back. Send that palomino back to Bannerman's ranch. I'll see that you get evened up for it."

"You damn well better."

The sheriff went toward the door. "Which way did he head, Sid? And don't lie to me."

"Due south."

Harry Greiff brought up the tired horses, and they moved saddles to Horn's relay string. McAffee marched up to the sheriff, rubbed his rump, and said, "Know what's riding on this, don't you?"

"I know it as well as you do," the sheriff said.

"Election's one week from today," McAffee said. He scratched the tufted stubble on his cheek. "If you've got the Nigra back in jail by next Tuesday, you'll get reelected. If you haven't—" and he let it hang in the air.

Dinwiddie, listening on the fringes, finished for him: "If you haven't, Farris, I wouldn't give too much for your future in politics." He tried to make a joke of it, but his face was wan.

The sheriff ignored both of them. He spoke to Harry Greiff.

"We've got a norther coming up, Mr. Greiff. We'll try to cover as much ground as we can before it catches us. The prisoner has a six-hour head start. We'll try to pick up his tracks south of here."

Harry Greiff tugged a cinch up. He grunted while he spoke. "That's mighty open country out there to get caught in, sir."

"It's only October," the sheriff said. "I don't expect it to be much of a blizzard. It may be enough to make the prisoner take shelter, in which case we'll have a chance to close the gap between us. All set?"

"Yes, sir." Harry Greiff handed a pair of reins to the sheriff.

As always, the sheriff disregarded the unauthorized members of the posse. From the start, he had acted as if they weren't there. Clay had to invest great effort into tugging himself up onto the saddle. He spurred his horse to catch up with his father and the deputy. Behind him, McAffee and Dinwiddie milled around, trying to get on their horses. Temporarily revived, Clay urged the horse to a canter. In the station doorway Sid Horn watched them go. He had a towel against his face.

Harry Greiff moved ahead, prowling a rapid arc for prints. Clay's father reined back and said, "I'll only say this once, so listen to it. I had a feeling Ben was inside the station. He wasn't, but that's not what troubles me. It occurred to me that you were behind me with a gun—and I didn't trust you, boy. I can't have that. You'll turn your guns over to Mr. Greiff immediately, and you'll consider yourself under arrest. I'm holding myself accountable for your custody until we get home."

"Arrest? What for?"

"You and I both know there was only one person alive who could have let Ben out of jail with a key."

"Maybe he picked the lock," Clay suggested.

"If I'm wrong, I'll apologize when you prove it to my satisfaction."

"Guilty until proved innocent, hey?"

"Just don't get behind me, boy," his father said bleakly. "I wish to God I knew whose side you were on."

They were riding into a gathering midafternoon twilight. Tall lances of cloud shot forward from the unrolling crest of the storm. A chill sensation ruffled Clay's flesh. He bound his hat down around his ears with his bandanna, and he said, "If you had any brains, you'd know what side I'm on. I'm on your side, whether you know it or not. You are my father, aren't you?"

"Sometimes I'm not even sure of that anymore," the sheriff said.

"You should have let him go yourself. You wanted to. Ben wanted you to. We all wanted you to."

His father said, "The law doesn't make allowances for what a man wants to do, Clay," and pulled his horse away.

They covered two miles of ground, and a strange feeling rolled through Clay. The air was still. The crunching of the horses' feet was much louder than it should have been. Clay buckled on his oilskin rain slicker over the heavy coat. Harry Greiff had his rifle and revolver; Clay was weighted down by less impedimenta than the rest of them. Shaggy and surly, McAffee and Dinwiddie rode a little behind him, loosely straddling their horses and huddling against the cold. Out ahead, the two gray manhunters drummed on at a steady canter, covering stretched-out figure eights. The sheriff had found the tracks.

Dinwiddie said, "God must have had it in for this country. Christ, you'd think he'd get tired of chasing after his own pointed finger. I hanker for a soft bed and a warm fire and something I can get my teeth into."

"He'll never abandon the search," said McAffee. "The man's choking to death in the embrace of his ambition."

The sheriff called a halt and dismounted to scan the ground afoot. When the others caught up, he said, "Turned southwest here. He probably aimed for those buttes when he saw the storm coming up. It may be he'll take shelter from the wind there."

The buttes, just visible through the dark swirl of air, stood a good eighteen or twenty miles distant across the desert.

"He won't travel in a storm," the sheriff said, "not down here. He doesn't know the country."

McAffee said, "Shriveled guts and saddle sores. We're all used up, Farris. Can't fight our way through a blizzard—too damned exhausted. We'd better lay over and wait it out. He won't gain any ground on us."

"Nor us on him," the sheriff said. "We'll proceed."

McAffee unbuckled his saddlebag and brought forth his bottle of John Vale. Clay had watched him deplete several bottles. The supply seemed endless. McAffee said, "You'd ride us all into the ground to save your chance in this election, wouldn't you?"

"You're the one who wants to be sheriff," Farris Rand said. "Still liking the idea, McAffee?" He turned to his horse and settled his boot in the stirrup. "Turn back if you want to. You can still make Sid Horn's before the storm breaks." He lifted himself astride the horse and gigged it away.

Sometime in the next half hour Clyde Littlejack came bouncing along. Clay hadn't even noticed his absence, but when he thought about it, he realized he hadn't seen Littlejack for several hours. The farrier had the carcass of a whitetail doe sprawled across the packhorse saddle.

The sheriff looked back. "You make a hell of a man-hunter, Clyde."

"We've all got to eat." Fatigue had subdued Littlejack's bellicosity.

"Or don't you get hungry, either?" said Dinwiddie, who was beginning to display awe at the sheriff's monumental, unflagging endurance.

Overhead, the forming darkness pressed down. Clay's feet and exposed face felt the blades of the cold. The height of the jagged clouds told of a tremendous wind rushing forward. Dust devils appeared vaguely in the distance. Behind them marched a spreading darkness. The last of the day drained out of the sky: within an hour the wind's reverberation was a trembling, charging echo. It was like the distant drumming of a herd in full stampede.

The first touch of the wind disturbed the horses and put them into a nervous trot. The sheriff kept an uneasy watch on the black storm boiling ahead.

They closed within five miles of the buttes. The churning force rushed upon them, all wild crying and oblivion; Clay heard the roar of the norther in full fury. Pressure siezed him. It shook him on the saddle. It was a great voice howling. Slashing blades of snow and hail battered him. The sheriff and Harry Greiff herded them all together, and the sheriff tied a rope from bridle to bridle, linking them all together. The thrust of the wind made them angle sharply to stay on course. Clay scraped forming frost from his jaw and saw the moisture of his breath steaming swiftly away.

The time came when he could no longer see the ground at the horse's feet. What had been blackness became a swirl of white. His legs began to numb. He kicked them against the stirrups: the tingling that ran up his knees was almost pleasant. He huddled inside his clothes and batted his gloved hands together.

Something whacked his thigh. A hand reached up and tugged his sleeve. He bent down.

It was his father. "Get down and walk." The wind ripped the words away.

He climbed down and fixed his fist to the horse's headstall. His legs were all but unfeeling. His nose was stiff, cheeks raw, ears throbbing.

He battled forward against the wind, against panic. *Going in circles. Maybe we're going in circles. Does a blind man feel like this? Jesus—Jesus.*

The wind knocked him flat against the horse. The horse danced back. He leaned forty degrees into the wind and kept moving, tugged by the rope that disappeared ahead toward Harry Greiff's horse. His legs were wooden stalks by now, but it was his ears that really hurt. He took off one glove with his teeth and got his hand under his hat to rub his ears, one at a time. They began to burn.

The wind slacked. He believed he could see the misty shape of a horse ahead of him. They plodded another ten yards, and he recognized Harry Greiff's square back beyond that horse. In patchy glimpses he could make out his father.

The sheriff kept moving until the air was almost clear. He called a halt under the cliff of the butte.

They gathered around in a knot, striking each other's coats, puffing up clouds of snow. The sheriff said, "Don't sit down—don't quit moving. All of you stay put here. Mr. Greiff, you and I will scout the base of this mesa."

McAffee said, "For God's sake, have a rest, Farris."

"He may be within a hundred feet of us right this minute," said the sheriff. He slogged into the gloom with the deputy on his heels. Greiff stripped off his glove and lifted his revolver.

Afraid, Clay stood rooted for only a moment. He broke out of his tracks and went after them.

Chapter 21

THEY found no one.

The storm moved on as quickly as it had come. Sundown brought the last of the snowfall, though the wind kept on, strong enough to chill Clay through.

The sheriff assembled a council of war. McAffee was the first to speak. "We're dead on our feet, Farris—and so are you. Even if the Nigra stumbled into our midst right now, none of us would be able to hold him. Not even you. We've got to rest."

Harry Greiff said, "We can't find tracks now anyway, sir."

Clyde Littlejack was off in the dark somewhere; his howl came roaring forward.

"What the hell?" Clay said, spinning.

They set out at a run.

A cross of boards stood driven casually into the ground, right at the base of the cliff where the wind could not tear it up. Littlejack was kneeling down. He cupped a lighted match and played it across the face of the marker. There was a knife-scratched legend:

SHERIFF RAND 1841—1896

The sheriff's moustache was limp in the damp wind. He looked somber and tragic. The look he gave the loose weary men around him was disgusted. Harry Greiff regarded him glumly.

"All right," the sheriff said, without feeling. "I'll get him, Mr. Greiff. I always do."

Clay said, "Goddam it, he's your—"

"*Shut up!*" For a moment Clay believed his father was going to strike him. Then the sheriff dropped his arm. "That boy wiped his feet on me, Clay."

Harry Greiff ripped up the cross. He broke it across his knee and hurled the pieces into the night.

Farris Rand said, "Get mounted."

McAffee blinked. "Now?"

"Now. He can't travel in mud without leaving tracks. It's our chance to get him. Move!"

McAffee began to protest. Harry Greiff turned on him and began to bark like a master sergeant.

Clay had watched his father's face grow emptier day by day.

They camped without a fire and waited for dawn. Clay sank his teeth into the raw fresh venison. He almost gagged. With his portion half-eaten, he slumped back. Sleep struck him like a club.

There was rain. It woke him; daylight filtered weakly through the cold drizzle. His father was already mounted. Clay cinched up and cantered after him; the others straggled across a mile of desert.

From a ridge line they spotted a red-painted stagecoach pulled by four Kentucky mules. Half an hour later they stopped at the Council Springs crossroads store. The storekeeper had not seen a passing horseman, but the tracks went by there, only an hour old.

The trail of the single-shod horse led them south by southwest. Near noon it crossed the Prescott coach road. The drizzle started and stopped by fits, not laying down enough moisture to erase tracks. Heavier gray clouds scudded forward, cutting off the sun.

In thick, high grass Harry Greiff halted and stepped down to examine the ground where the pursued horse had wandered across a bare ant hill.

"Tracks been meandering," said Greiff. "Thought it was curious. Look here." He stood up, dusted his hands, and surveyed the horizons. "Something wrong, sir. These tracks ain't deep enough."

Farris Rand unsheathed his field glasses and raised them to his eyes. He swept the southward desert with slow care.

Harry Greiff said, "From the look of this, that horse has got no rider on him."

"I see it," the sheriff said. The field glasses steadied. "Grazing with the saddle still on him."

"Huh?" said Clyde Littlejack.

Clay said, "What?"

Harry Greiff pushed his hat back. "Reckon he dismounted at the coach road and slapped the horse on."

Dinwiddie said, "That'd take a lot of nerve."

"He's got a lot of nerve," said the sheriff. "He knows we're tight behind him. He decided to risk it, that's all."

"I don't get it," Clay said. "It doesn't add up."

Harry Greiff said, "He drove the horse away and waited in the road for somebody to come by and pick him up."

"Somebody? Somebody who?"

"Who knows. Maybe he boarded that stagecoach we saw."

McAffee said, "But that coach was headed north."

"He might have done that," the sheriff observed, "just to throw us off the scent. With a little more luck he'd have had us waste half the day down here with our noses to the ground."

It took them twenty minutes to backtrack to the coach road. The sheriff and his deputy dismounted to inspect the earth. After a while Harry Greiff straightened up with a grunt. "Deep bootprints here, sir. He squatted for a while, waiting."

Dinwiddie said, "He could have gone either way. Too much traffic in those ruts—they'd swallow up any tracks."

"To be sure," said the sheriff. He went back to his horse and climbed up. "If he went south, he'd have had to walk. There hasn't been a southbound coach along today. If he went north, then he's on that coach we passed."

Greiff said, "He's just shrewd enough to walk on south and lay back off the road somewhere down in those hills."

Littlejack said, "He'd get a lot farther on the stage."

The sheriff was considering it. Colonel McAffee said, "Just for the sake of argument—"

"Which I don't need at all right now."

"—let's say he did take the stagecoach. Where does that put him? Prescott? Your telegram's in the sheriff's office there. The Nigra's too easy to recognize. He wouldn't take that chance."

Harry Greiff said, "He could have gotten off the stage any place between here and Prescott."

The sheriff spoke slowly. "He's on the run. He's scared. His first instinct will be to put miles behind him."

McAffee said, "Counted the ifs in that, Farris? It's a long shot."

"It's the only shot we've got. I'd suggest we shoot it."

Ben was not on the coach, had never been on it, had not been seen by the driver. It was late afternoon by then, but Farris Rand spoke calmly. "All right. He's gained eight hours, but he has no horse and it will take him a day's walking to reach the nearest ranch. We're going after him."

Dinwiddie regarded him with wry bemusement. "Looks like he put one over on you, Farris. I believe it's the first time I ever saw you get slickered."

"Then cherish the memory," Rand said. "You won't have many like it."

"Oh, I don't know about that," Dinwiddie remarked.

Clay looked out from under his lowered hatbrim at the blur of the land ahead. Fatigue drove agony through him. Rain pelted the ground with steadily increasing pressure; it leaked down his neck, soaked through his pants, logged his gloves, runneled down before his face from the trough of his hatbrim.

He almost capsized when the horse stopped.

He lifted his head drunkenly. Ahead of him the others had halted. Dinwiddie's drawl swam into his awareness:

". . . ends it. You can't find tracks now. This will wash them all out."

Littlejack uttered a monosyllabic curse. Clay took off his hat. He closed his eyes and threw his head back. Rain dashed his face. He ran his fingers through strands of disheveled hair, replaced the glove on his hand and sat hatless. Rain soaked his head.

"He challenged the law," the sheriff said. "He will not get away."

Clay formed a loose fist and put his hat on.

He saw his father's gravely wooden face through the rain. McAffee said, "Enough. Enough of this madness. A man with sense knows when to accept the inevitable."

Dinwiddie said, "In a temporary seizure of insanity, we decided to ride with you, Farris. But the game's all done. For Christ's sake, Farris—"

"Go back," the sheriff said. "All of you go back if you want. I'm going on."

"I believe I'm your man," Harry Greiff muttered, and moved his horse closer to the sheriff's.

McAffee said, "You won't get him back. Not by Tuesday morning."

"I'll get him back if it takes all winter, Colonel."

McAffee swallowed a drink and corked his bottle. "I don't believe you will, Farris. At any rate I've had enough. I'm going home. Anybody going with me?"

"I, for one," said Dinwiddie. He had lost his stovepipe hat in the storm; his hair was matted. "I'm sorry, Farris. I'll keep my mouth shut."

"What?" said Littlejack.

Dinwiddie said, "What about you, Clyde?"

"Hell, I got a business to run. I'm goin' home."

"All those trails leading nowhere." Dinwiddie shook his head sadly. "You're a foolish man, Farris."

McAffee said, "You're all through in Ocotillo."

"I am not all through, gentlemen, until next Tuesday, and at that point it's a matter of conscience for all of you. Just remember who abandoned the law when the trail began to cool—and who did not. You'll feel a bit silly when I bring the prisoner into town Tuesday morning."

"Farris," said Dinwiddie, "you are incredible. If I had my hat, I'd take it off to you. But you're still a Goddam fool." He neck-reined his horse around and spurred it to a lope, heading north.

Littlejack said, "You get that Nigra, Farris, you give him a couple bullets for me, hey? Come on, Colonel."

McAffee searched the sheriff's face. For some reason that Clay sensed but did not understand, McAffee's flaccid hand reached out. The sheriff gave him a short, hard handshake, and McAffee rode away, jouncing.

"Let's move on, then," said the sheriff.

Time and failure had pared the posse down to these three. They came across a place where some hopeful hard-rocker had tried to strike it rich; they passed on. Clay thought fitfully of Lavender—the way her eyebrows peaked up when she was earnest, the way she tossed her head when she laughed, the quiet warmth of her hazel eyes.

His jaw was slurred by a light beard. He had developed deep vertical creases between his brows. His face was whacked and burned into a leather mask, and his mouth was bracketed by brittle lines. The mark of fatigue had settled into his face as though it were indelible.

The wind carried light snowflakes in a powder-dusting. Just after dark they raised the lights of a lonely dwelling, below in a long dish of land. They rode forward. He saw his father take off his gloves and flex his fingers.

A parchment-faced old woman stood in front of the hut, watching them come up.

" 'Noches," said the sheriff. His voice was a dry rasp.

The woman neither moved nor spoke. A man came out, a shrunken old Indian, scrawny with a potbelly.

"Somos amigos," said the sheriff.

"Seguro que sí," the old man said, sardonically. *Sure you are.*

The old man's cyanotic hands fiddled with his shirt. The sheriff said, "Está que ustedes hayan visto un Negro sobre un caballo bayo?"

The old man said, "Su amigo?"

"Es un ladron."

"He lo visto," the old Indian said.

The sheriff said, "They've seen him."

"When?" Clay said. "How long ago? Which way was he headed?"

The sheriff translated; the old Indian began to talk. He recounted all his ailments and the difficulties of his existence. "I am a man with many hurts."

The sheriff said carefully in Spanish, "There is always sadness. There is no life without sorrows."

"He went away to the south. *Está por allá.*"

"Gracias."

"Vaya con fortuna," said the old man. "I hope you kill the *ladron.*"

Under a pewter midmorning sky they halted the horses to breathe them. All night it had been a search for shadows.

The horse ahead had pulled up lame, and the tracks were fresh.

Harry Greiff murmured to Clay, "Take your gloves off, son. A mistake like that can get you killed."

"I've got no gun, anyway."

"Uh. Forgot that."

The sheriff held up his hand; they halted near a grove. They all heard it then: the soft thudding footfall of a horse browsing for forage.

Sweat was sticky in the small of Clay's back, in his palms, in his crotch, on his lips and throat. It was a chilly day.

The sheriff said, "Could be a lot of people besides Ben passing through this way. But take care."

They rode from tree to tree, through a thick growth of spring-fed brush and cottonwoods. An overwhelming anxiety poisoned Clay's remaining patience.

They found the horse unsaddled and freed. It was hobbling on three legs.

"It'll heal," said Greiff after inspecting the horse. "But he's on foot now. Less than an hour. That way."

Clay's heart raced. His anger kindled, he shouted at his father: "How do you expect to give him his law and order? In the belly or right between the eyes?"

His father's knuckles whitened around the reins. He made no answer. Harry Greiff said, "That boy Ben will keep going until they put him in jail or in a grave."

Clay's father said, "Clay, you're going to have to learn to stop asking questions that have no answers. You play the cards that are dealt you, that's all."

Harry Greiff broke in. His voice had no more feeling than if he were describing the weather. "That's him up yonder, I reckon."

Diminutive by distance, the figure of a man walked across the desert flats.

"Ben," said Clay.

The sheriff lifted his horse to a lope.

Ben Harmony stopped and turned full around to face them, both hands empty. The sheriff jammed his horse to a bruising halt that spewed dirt clots.

The sheriff's mouth worked.

Ben Harmony said, "You look like you haven't slept in weeks."

"Been a long time since I closed both eyes," the sheriff said. "How are you, boy?"

"Still taking nourishment. Maybe footsore some. Hello, Chico, I didn't expect to see you this soon."

Clay brought his horse up and stopped. "Ben—"

The sheriff said, "You'll be pretty hungry, I imagine. Mr. Greiff, let's start a fire." He stepped down. "I'll take your guns, boy."

"I didn't figure you'd find me till I was ready to be found," Ben said. "You're pretty good, old man." He unslung the rifle off his back and handed it over; he gave over his gun-belted revolver as well. "I guess there are some things you just can't change, and you're one of them. Going to take me back?"

"I believe I am," said the sheriff.

Harry Greiff was away gathering fuel. Clay said in a taut, small voice, "You'll do it, too, won't you?"

"Did you ever doubt me?" his father said. His gaze swiveled toward the southern horizon, and he said to Ben Harmony, "Do you know where you are right now?"

"Not exactly."

"Less than a mile from the Mexican border," the sheriff said. He pointed with his arm and let it drop. "You almost did it, boy."

"Hard luck, then. If I'd known that, I'd have run just a little bit faster. But like Mr. Lincoln said, if you can't make a mistake, you can't make anything. You've made a few yourself, old man."

Harry Greiff built a fire. "First hot food we've seen," he said. "Four days to go, sir. I reckon we can still make it back by election time."

"Yes," the sheriff said. He squatted by the fire and held out his palms.

Ben saw Clay regarding the guns hung on Harry Greiff's saddle. Ben said, "I wouldn't think about that, Chico."

"I'm in a pretty wild mood right now," said Clay.

The sheriff said, "I want to talk to both of you. Mr. Greiff, leave us alone."

"Yes, sir." Harry Greiff got up and went back to the

horses. Clay followed Ben Harmony to the fire, and the sheriff pointed at the ground.

They sat. The sheriff said, "I guess there are a lot of things wrong with me."

"Have been for a long time," said Ben Harmony.

"Am I supposed to forget what you did to Shoumacher?"

"What did I do to Shoumacher?" Ben Harmony demanded. "I'll tell you something, old man. I hit him once on the chin and he tripped over his own feet trying to get away from me. Hit his head on the printing press and knocked the lamp down. You call that murder?"

"Don't tell me. It's not a decision for me to make."

"Sure," said Ben Harmony. "It's a decision for a white jury, isn't it?"

The sheriff said, "I'd like to hold out an olive branch, boy. I wish I could do that."

"Suit yourself," Ben said. "I don't aim to get on my knees and beg you to make peace."

The wind buffeted Clay's ears and made his hatbrim flap. His father's black-booted feet stirred in the dust. It was a shock for Clay to look into those red eyes deep in his father's skull. It was as if a stopper had fallen from place and all the sand had run out.

"You're just another outlaw, boy."

"Reckon I am," Ben Harmony agreed. "What are you trying to talk yourself into, old man?"

Clay said quickly to his father, "Today means more than yesterday."

"Nothing's changed," his father said.

Clay said, "You've gone sour as vinegar."

"There are a lot of things I wanted to say to both of you. Now the time's come and I don't know how. Christ, don't you think I want to turn the leaf? I'm a lawman, a Goddam lawman."

"There's law," Clay said, "and then there's justice."

"And there's my son," said Farris Rand. "Both my sons. You are both my sons."

Ben Harmony said, "What?"

"You are both my sons," the sheriff said again, slowly and distinctly. He put his face down, as if to shield it from the wind. "Some things can burn the soul out of you."

Ben Harmony was stretching his legs out along the

ground, leaning back as if he were enjoying the looseness that might follow a big meal. He said, "Take me back if you want to. It'll be all right now."

"Because I said what you wanted to hear me say?"

"That was all I ever wanted from you," said Ben Harmony.

Clay said in heat, "If Ben goes back to Ocotillo, he'll hang. That hasn't changed."

"You're both my sons," his father roared. "I ask you to trust me."

"Why," said Ben Harmony, "we can do that. What do you say, Chico?"

"What's going to happen?" Clay asked.

His father said, "What do you want to happen? I wish to God you'd stop looking at me like some kind of stranger, Clay."

The sheriff stood up fast. He took an oilskin pouch from inside his coat and unwrapped it to remove a dry cigar. His fine white teeth flickered. He lighted up and said, "I need to have a few words with Mr. Greiff. I'd be obliged if you two would wait for me." He took three paces away and paused; he said over his shoulder, "The border is one mile south of here," and walked on to the horses.

Ben Harmony said, "Well, Chico?"

"If you make a run for it, he'll turn himself in. You know he will."

"No," Ben Harmony said. "He told us to wait for him, didn't he?"

He got up and began walking south.

Baffled, Clay looked toward his father. The sheriff was talking to his deputy, having maneuvered around so that in order to face him, Harry Greiff had to put his back to the fire. The cigar gestured up and down in the sheriff's grip.

Clay trotted after Ben Harmony. He caught up and looked back. "Listen, we didn't think about this."

"I thought about it."

"He's got to throw away thirty years. He'll be an outlaw himself."

"I thought about it," Ben Harmony said again, and walked on.

The fence was rusty and sagging. Clay put his boot on the

middle barbwire strand and lifted the top wire. Ben Harmony stooped and slipped through. He stood up and said, "We wait here."

"He'll turn himself in, Ben. I know him. He'll spend five years in jail for this."

"Maybe he won't."

The sheriff and Greiff came over the rise on horseback, leading the third horse. The sheriff said, "Your wirecutters, Mr. Greiff."

Clay said, "What's that for?"

The deputy got down and clamped his cutters around the top strand. The wire broke with a crack and went singing away down the fence; the curled ends whipped back. Greiff bent down to sever the remaining strands.

The sheriff said, "Mr. Greiff, I've made myself a fugitive and I can't give you orders. I make a personal request, as a friend. Ride through the fence with me."

"Yes, sir," Harry Greiff said, without remark. He put away his wirecutters, got on his horse and moved it forward. The two horsemen came through the break. The sheriff said, "Leave a horse behind, Mr. Greiff."

"Sir?"

"Clay won't be coming with us."

Clay's mind had closed up; it wasn't making sense of things.

The sheriff said, "You've got a ranch to run and a woman to think of. She's too fine a woman to be left alone."

"I never thought about leaving her alone. But I'll go with you. I'll send for her. She'll come, you'll see. Look, I did break Ben out of jail—it was my crime, too. Let me come."

"Go on home," his father said. "It's your home, it belongs to you. It doesn't belong to us anymore. You've got roots—don't tear them up."

"But I—"

"Do what he wants, Chico," Ben Harmony said. "It's what I want, too."

His father said, "When you see your mother, tell her—" The sheriff took the cigar out of his mouth. He had bitten it cleanly in two. "Tell her your brother and I went prospecting in Sonora."

The sheriff extended his arm. Ben Harmony gripped it and swung himself up behind the sheriff.

Clay moved like a sleepwalker, up to his father. He shook hands with both of them and said lamely, "Good luck to you."

"Take care of yourself, Chico."

His father said, "You may have to give McAffee a hand. Treat him kindly. Treat yourself kindly, boy."

The horse wheeled away, packing double. Clay stood by the fence while Harry Greiff trotted past, tugging down his hat by the brim. Greiff yelled, "So long, son," and spurred to catch up.

Clay did not move for a quarter of an hour. He saw them climb over a distant rise. Ben Harmony's hat—it was Clay's own hat; he had given it to Ben—lifted and waved.

They were gone. He walked over to the cigar his father had thrown away. He picked it up and went to his horse. He got mounted and adjusted the reins.

"The hell," he said. He threw the cigar away, glanced once to the south, and turned his back on Mexico.